Love, Lust
& Everything in Between

Love, Lust
& Everything in Between

Cassandra Jefferson

Library of Congress Control Number:		2009913874
ISBN:	Hardcover	978-1-4535-7884-1
	Softcover	978-1-4535-7883-4

To order additional copies of this book, contact:
Xlibris Corporation
1-888-795-4274
www.Xlibris.com
Orders@Xlibris.com
69114

Chapter 1

It had been six months since Virgil's husband, Steve, left. He's in the music business and tours a lot. Usually, Virgil went along, but because of their beautiful new addition to the family made it kind of hard to keep up, so Virgil decided to sit this one out.

Every day was becoming pretty much the same for Virgil. Her day began at seven in the morning with duties that included: feeding April, changing her, taking her out for a stroll, putting her down for a nap, and starting all over again.

Virgil was so used to being around Steve all of the time that it was very upsetting for her to be bored. She was getting tired of the same old everyday lifestyle. Virgil wanted more to her life than just staying at home and babysitting. Virgil loved April very much, but she wasn't willing to give up the lifestyle to which she'd became accustomed.

One day, as Virgil was staring out of her double-wide living room window as she did every day about noon, the telephone rang. Virgil ran to the phone, hoping it was Steve.

"Hello," said Virgil calmly, trying not to sound out of breath.

"What's up?" said the voice on the other end.

"Oh, it's you," said Virgil, disappointed that it wasn't Steve.

"He-ee-y! Did I catch you at a bad time or something?"

"No, Liza, I'm sorry. I just thought you were Steve. I haven't heard from him in three days."

"Oh, don't worry. I'm sure he's all right," said Liza, trying to cheer up the conversation.

"I just want to know whether he made it there safely or not. He could have called me and told me something so I don't have to worry so much."

"Well, maybe he'll call later. We can just hope for the best. You know, Virgil, I was thinking, since you're not doing anything tonight, I thought maybe we could go out, like old times. You know, like before you and I became married women."

"Liza, that sounds like a good idea, but what about April?"

"What about her? You know Mom would just love to watch April for you."

"I know she would, but April is so small and I don't want Mom to be nervous about keeping her."

"Come on, Virgil, you are making up excuses."

"Okay, I guess I am. I'll go out with you. What time are you picking me up?"

"Seven o'clock."

"Okay, seven sounds good."

After the phone call, Virgil felt guilty. Looking down at April and brushing back her hair, Virgil leaned down close to her ear and whispered softly, "Daddy will be home soon, sweetheart, don't you worry." Then she slowly turned her head towards the window, unsure of what she'd just said.

After showering, Virgil stood in front of her closet, looking endlessly for something to wear. After about an hour or putting on one thing then taking off another, she finally found a pair of black slacks and a black-and-white blouse with the flared sleeves.

She looked into the mirror, at her short but slender body and was very pleased at what she saw. As soon as she ran into the bathroom to do that last touch-up on her makeup, she heard the honking of Liza's car horn.

Virgil ran to get into Liza's car. "Why are you here so early, girl? I was still putting on my makeup, girlfriend," she said, hitting Liza on the arm.

"Oh, excuse me, Witch Hazel. Sorry to disturb you."

"And just who are you calling witch hazel?—with your bride of 'Frankenstein hairstyle?"

"Oh no, that's not right," said Liza, laughing at the joke. "You better fell lucky that you caught me off guard with that one."

The club, was very crowded. It was ladies' night, and there were more men than women. The men were there early so they could get the women to buy their drinks for them. Since they were sold for only one dollar for the ladies until midnight.

Liza spotted her common law husband. Who practically dragged her out onto the dance floor while she screamed back to Virgil. "Order drinks!"

"Order drinks? I don't know how to order drinks, said Virgil to herself. The only thing that I know how to order is a daiquiri and alcoholics don't drink daiquiris."

As Virgil pushed her way through the crowd, she finally made it to the bar. She looked around at all the different kinds of bottles and it made her confused.

"May I help you, Miss?" said the bartender. Virgil looked in the direction of the voice, and saw a tall, dark, and very handsome man. He was all of that and more.

Virgil, was trying not to stare and she replied, "Well, I'm new at this. My sister told me to order drinks and I haven't the slightest idea what to order. I want to try something new, something that I can handle without making a face."

The bartender looked at Virgil and smiled. "For a pretty lady like you, I prefer myself. Hello, my name is Kirk . . . and your name is?"

"It's Virgil."

"Well, nice to meet you, Virgil, and guess what? I have a daughter named Virgil and she's beautiful, just like you," said Kirk as he grabbed her hand and kissed it.

"So how old is your daughter?"

"She is three years old and going on thirty." They both laughed.

"Well, are you married?"

Kirk hesitated for a moment, then replied, "No, my wife died minutes after my daughter was born."

"Oh, I'm so sorry."

"That's okay. Things will get better with time. Well, I tell you what, Virgil, I just thought about the perfect drink for you and your sis. It's a specialty of mine, try it out and tell me what you think."

Kirk quickly made the drinks for Virgil and set them on the counter. Virgil took the drinks and on a napkin underneath was his phone number.

Virgil looked at Kirk and smiled. She set the drinks back down on the counter and put the number in her pants pocket, she then looked around and spotted John and Liza right away. She picked up the drinks and walked over to them. Liza yelled, "What took you so long? "I saw you over there being fresh with that good-looking bartender."

John gave Liza a little push. "Just kidding, honey," said Liza, giving John a big hug.

As the night went on, Liza kept giving John goo-goo eyes and feeling the front of his pants, sending his blood pressure sky-high. Virgil was having fun dancing in front of the bar so she could look at Kirk all night.

As Virgil left the floor, she noticed that John and Liza were nowhere in sight. She started to panic, then she decided that she'd begin looking for them and if she couldn't find them, then she'd panic.

First, she looked in the restroom. No Liza. Then she went to the car. No Liza. Looking all around, Virgil saw a flight of stairs. 'Why didn't I think of looking up there at first?'

When Virgil made it to the top of the stairs and combed the room, she saw Liza and John in one of the corners where the light was dim but one could still tell who they were.

They were kissing, as usual, and John's hand was up Liza's skirt an probably up her cunt as well, while Liza was fondling around with John's tool.

Virgil moved behind the pole in front of them so she could get a better view, but it was too late.

Liza jumped up and said, "Oh, Virgil, I didn't see you coming."

Virgil giggled. "Well, that's understandable. How could you when your mouth was full and your hands were busy?" "I think you two should go home before you get busted for indecent exposure."

"Oh no, Virgil, I'm here so you can have a goo time."

"That's okay, I'm ready to go. Besides, Steve might call me."

"I rode with a friend," said John. "Would it be okay if you dropped us off at my house and you can take Liza's car home?"

"Okay," said Virgil. "Sounds good."

Reaching the car, Liza and John dashed for the back seat. "Don't worry, guys, I'll drive," said Virgil, giving them one of her mean looks. "I'm not your chauffeur," she said sarcastically.

As soon as the car started to move, John put his hands under Liza's skirt and removed her panties. Liza moaned in excitement, and in return, she unzipped John's jeans. Virgil got a cold chill when she heard the sound of John's zipper.

Liza started fondling John's big cock. He was getting so excited that he pushed Liza's head down to give him the big blow. Virgil had to stop for a train, so now she could get a better view.

Looking in the mirror, she saw Liza's head going up and down on John's thick, juicy rod.

"Oh Gosh! said Virgil to herself. I don't know how much of this that I can take. If they keep this up, I think I'm going to come on myself. And since it's been six months since I've seen a cock close-up, this is just driving me insane."

Soon Liza stopped sucking John's cock and started doing something that Virgil had never seen her do before. John turned on his knees, sticking his nice round ass straight into the air facing Liza while she licked away at his hole.

"Now I'm going to wreck," said Virgil, out loud. John was squealing with excitement while Liza struggled to keep her grip. Soon, Virgil pulled into their driveway.

"The truck stops here, assholes," Virgil said with a grin. John and Liza hopped out of the car without even fixing their clothes, they got out as is. Liza's breasts were hanging out of her shirt, and John's cock was hanging huge out of his pants—, it was shiny and swollen all at the same time.

Virgil swallowed hard at the sight of it. Even out of the car and in public, they were still going at each other.

"See you guys later, okay?" They didn't hear Virgil as they fondled each other into the house. "Man," said Virgil, "I can't believe how turned on I am as her eyes followed the horny couple as they disappeared inside.

She sat there for a minute before she looked down at her watch, and realized that it was one o'clock already. 'Kirk gets off at one-thirty,' she recalled. She drove back to the club hoping to catch him before he left. Just as she was walking back inside, of the club, Kirk was coming out.

"I was coming back to see if you wanted to go somewhere quiet and have some breakfast or something," said Virgil in a very shy voice.

"Why, sure! he replied. I was hoping that you'd come back since you didn't say good-bye when you left. Follow me," said Kirk. "We'll go to my place. I cook a mean omelet."

Upon Virgil's arrival at Kirk's place, he exited his truck first and motioned for her to pull her car into his garage. When Virgil walked into Kirk's domain. "Wow!" she exclaimed. "You have a very nice place. This is amazing."

"Why, thank you. but I have to say, under the circumstances, I wouldn't have gotten any of this if it wasn't for my wife dying and all. To be honest with you, and you'll probably find this hard to believe, but I haven't really dated anyone since my wife died.

I tried it, but every time that I would go out with other women, a guilty feeling will arouse within me, which made me feel like I was betraying my wife.

Virgil gave him an understanding look, but said nothing.

But now I'm slowly becoming myself again. I decided that I must move on, so I bought this house with the insurance money so that my daughter will have something to hold on to if I pass away.

I'm still having a problem with Holidays. Maybe they will ease up in time."

Virgil felt kind of sorry for him, so she went over and put her arms around him. "If you want to cry, you can use my shoulder," she said as she held him tight.

"You know what, Virgil, I think I'm all out of tears. It just feels good to hug someone every once in a while." Kirk slowly raised Virgil's head, bent over and kissed her full on the mouth. Virgil responded by sticking her tongue between his lips.

Kirk pulled away, looking deep into Virgil's eyes.

"I don't know what it is, but for some reason, there is something about you that makes it feel right. I mean, for some reason, I don't feel guilty.

Actually, I feel comfortable around you, and this is the same feeling that I got when I touched your hand in the club."

Virgil blushed.

"And that smile of yours can really turn a person on. It's like you have special powers or something." He (walked around her) stopping behind her, and checked out her ass.

"What are you doing?" asked Virgil, trying not to sound bashful.

"I'm staring at your beautiful round ass." Kirk slowly rubbed Virgil's shoulders, then cautiously slid his hands down until he got to the good part, grabbing her ass with both hands.

"Move over to the mirror so that I can get a good look at you," said Kirk in a very kinky way. Standing in front of the mirror, Kirk started to remove Virgil's clothes, starting with her shoes then her slacks first.

He tossed them aside, he stood behind her, holding her around her waist as if she were to run away. He was so close that Virgil could feel the large bulge on the right side of his paper-thin slacks.

It felt so good that Virgil couldn't wait until he slide his big soft hands down her panties. Her thought was no more because as soon as it ended, Kirk was running his big strong hands over her breasts and down to her eager-waiting clit.

Virgil moaned with excitement. Kirk turned her around and slowly unbuttoned her blouse, throwing it over to the side with the slacks. He picked her up and carefully took the stairs that led to his bedroom.

Once in the room, he placed her on a big black furry bear rug. As Virgil looked around she noticed that almost everything in the room was either black or red. It was nicely decorated; it even had a red light bulb in the ceiling.

The fireplace was already a blaze with a nice warm fire making flickers of light on Virgil's nearly nude body. Kirk stood before Virgil and slowly started removing his clothes, beginning with his shoes and socks first, then reaching for his shirt and slowly pulling it over his head, showing his muscled, hairy chest.

Virgil's eyes widened. Kirk noticed the expression on her face, so he tossed his shirt so that it would almost hit her between the legs. He opened the top part of his slacks and unzipped the zipper so that his pants would just drop to the floor.

Virgil thought that she would faint when she saw that he didn't have on any underwear. His cock was huge, and it jumped out like a jack-in-the-box in a birthday suit.

Virgil's eyes couldn't help but follow as Kirk dropped down to his knees in front of her, looking into her eyes. "Do you like what you see?" he asked in his hypnotizing voice.

Virgil leaned forward a little to get a better look. "Yes, I love what I see."

Kirk began by licking her hair, then slowly moved his tongue down her forehead and onto her neck, kissing both sides of them with a small nibble in between. Virgil moaned, so Kirk lingered in that spot on her neck to tease her just a little longer.

When Virgil begin to moan louder, he moved on by trailing his tongue to her ears, he licked around them, making her squirm a little. Kirk then made his tongue very pointed and began moving it in and out of Virgil's ear in a slow, fucking movement.

This made Virgil open her legs wide as she moved her head from side to side, trying to get away from the tingle of Kirk's touch, but he held a firm. Grip. "Handle it, baby, handle it," he whispered.

Kirk noticed that Virgil was getting very turned on by him, so he raised up and straddled her, giving her a little push so that her head fell gently onto the bear rug.

He grabbed both of Virgil's hands and held them above her head. He then began to rub his rock-hard penis over her face, across her lips, under her neck, up and down her stomach to her belly button, and down between her legs. Where he started humping up and down and moving in a sexy circle, barely touching her, still on his tease trip.

Virgil tried to free herself, but it was no use. Kirk's grip was too firm for her. "Feels good, doesn't it, baby? You want this dick, don't you?" he asked, as he kept the same pace.

"Yes, I do, so why are you making me wait?" asked Virgil as she raised her head to look Kirk in his face.

"Because I like a woman to beg for it," he said as he unsnapped Virgil's bra and slipped off her panties with one hand.

"Beg!" said Virgil. "I don't have to beg anyone."

"You will," he said.

Virgil was beginning to say something else, but was cut off by the tingling sensation of Kirk's lips on her fully erect nipples. Virgil's nipples tingled so much that she arched her back and threw her legs up into the air, and began to finger herself.

"I'll do that," said Kirk positioning himself between Virgil's eagerly awaiting thighs, not to mention her now—overly wet pussy. Kirk started out by licking her inner thighs and up to her fucking hole, driving her wild.

"Lick my clit! Lick my clit!" she screamed.

Kirk licked Virgil's clit like a strawberry lollipop and Virgil's hips bucked wildly. "I'm coming! I'm comi-n-g!" she said pushing his head closer to her ocean-flooded hole.

Kirk managed to break free. "Open your legs as wide as you can get them. I want to see how much cum is in your pussy," said Kirk, letting down a hard swallow. Virgil opened her legs.

"Your pussy is so wet," he said putting his finger inside her juices, then withdrawing it and licking his finger clean. Turn over, baby."

Virgil turned over on her knees, sticking her ass as far as it could go into the air.

"Ooohh," said Kirk watching as Virgil moved her ass round and round in that come-and-get-it way.

"Lick my ass, Kirk, please lick my ass for me."

Kirk grabbed hold of each of Virgil's cheeks, pulling them apart. He then teased her tiny hole by circling around it with his long wet tongue.

All f a sudden, without warning, he rammed his tongue into Virgil's asshole. Virgil was enjoying it too as she moved her ass around to keep up with his beat. Soon, juices stared flowing out of Virgil's asshole. "Fuck me, fuck this pussy."

Before Virgil could say another word, Kirk's hard pole was way up Virgil's hot pussy. He was going at her like a madman from hell.

"Whose pussy is this?" asked Kirk, still banging away.

"What?" Virgil whispered.

Kirk slapped Virgil on the ass. "I said, whose pussy is this?"

That caught her off guard. Virgil thought for a moment. "It's your pussy."

"I can't hear you," he said as he slapped her harder.

"It's your pussy!" yelled Virgil.

"Right answer," said Kirk, pulling his cock out just a little to tease her. Virgil tried to scoot back o get what she just lost, but Kirk grabbed her hips and said, "You didn't answer me loud enough the first time, so now you will have to be punished."

He started to spank her on her nice, tender ass again. Virgin gave out a scream of pleasure. Kirk took his steamy hot dick completely out of her wide-opened snatch and begin to slide it up and down her back as well as spanking her on her nice, ass with it.

Virgil started to beg. "Please give it to me, I'll be good. I'll do anything that you want."

"Anything?" asked Kirk.

"Yes, anything," said Virgil, putting her fingers inside of her cunt to get some juices then licking them.

"Okay," said Kirk. "I'll remember that." Kick flipped her over and started banging her again. Fucking her at what it seemed like fifty mph. Virgil was screaming, "Work that pussy! Make it come!"

Kirk gripped Virgil's hips tighter, and began to moan and fuck Virgil so hard that he could hardly keep up with himself. But, just when he thought he was going to lose some cum again, he slowed down to one of his famous circular movements, hitting that G-spot just right, and sliding his powerful hands over Virgil's body to make sure that she doesn't miss a tingle.

"How's that dick, Virgil? Uh? was her reply. Is that dick good to you?"

"Yes," she said making sure that she said it loud enough this time. "Yes, it's very good to me, so please fuck me a little harder, Master," she said with a greedy grin on her face.

Kirk didn't say a word. He slowly moved his hands from under her soft tender back, placing both hands flat on the rug. Raising up on both knees, he grabbed Virgil's legs, lifting her curved ass off the rug and began fucking her at full speed again.

"I see you like this dick long and hard, don't you?"

Before she could answer, that question, he ordered her turn over onto her side. Now, in the back of Virgil's mind, she was thinking, 'this is my kind of man, one that can go on and on and won't stop until I beg him to.'

Kirk mounted her and begin moving his cock around inside of her in a way that she'd never felt before in her life. With every move, he left a tingling sensation that sent the shivers up and down her spine.

Virgil then began to worry about being dickwhipped and in a situation that she couldn't get out of. Her thoughts were interrupted by that sexy moan that Kirk made.

"Your pussy feels god," he whispered. "Would you like for me to come all over you?"

"Give it to me, boy," she said in that kinky voice of hers. Kirk picked up speed again. Virgil felt as if she was in another time zone, her head was going up and down so fast that she just closed her eyes and let it all hang out.

'This shit is unbelievably good,' she thought. 'I feel like I've been smoking a joint or something.' Just when Virgil thought she was as high as she could get, Kirk put both of her legs over his shoulders and pounded her until they both came into a gushing climax.

He immediately put Virgil's legs gently onto the soft rug and laid on top of her, holding her for dear life. "Virgil, you just don't know how much I needed to release all of that pressure off my chest. Everything that was locked up inside of me is out in the open now.

I feel like a new person. I always wanted to know how it felt to say and do all of those things that I did tonight. I've always thought of it in the back of my mind, but just never did it. I don't know what came over me."

"You know, Kirk, I've never had a workout like that in my whole life. Do you know when you turned me over, I thought that we were finished, but to my surprise, the game was only beginning. I was thinking to myself, boy, am I in for it."

So tell me, how did you learn how to hold it like that?"

Virgil rolled over onto her side to see the expression on Kirk's face as he answered her question, she then noticed that he was fast asleep. After leaning over and giving him a big fat kiss on the cheek. She quietly go dressed, left a thank-you note, and her phone number on the table and she left.

Once at home, Virgil looked at her watch. It was now six o'clock.

"Six o'clock!" she screamed. "We were at it for about four hours nonstop. What a man!" she said out loud ripping off her clothes to prepare for a foggy hot shower. Pulling off her blouse and smelling it, Virgil noticed that it still had his scent on it.

"Mmmmmmm". Was her response, as she rubbed the blouse all over her body, down between her legs, and moved it back and forth across her still-aching clit.

After her shower, she laid across the bed staring into space, and fell asleep thinking about Kirk.

R-r-r-r! The telephone rang twice before she picked it up.

"Hello! Virgil?" said the voice on the other end. "Where in the hell have you been? I've been calling you since three o'clock."

"Well, it's kind of a long story, and I'm quite sure that you don't have time to hear it, so good-bye," said Virgil, trying to be sarcastic.

"Wait!" screamed Liza, very loudly. "Don't you dare hang up this phone, girl. I want to know where you took your little fast ass to."

"Okay, if you really want to know," said Virgil, trying not to sound too eager. "Well, I went back to the club last night to catch up with that nice bartender."

"You did what?" yelled Liza.

"Yes, it's true. You heard right. I went back to the club last night, ran into Kirk, and we went back to his place. He gave me a workout that I'll never forget. As a matter of fact, I can still feel his big round hard dick inside of me right now."

"Oh shit, Virgil! You had better be glad that I have to take John to work or else I'd demand to know every detail, but that's enough to hold me for now.

Well, don't go to sleep, because I'll be calling you as soon as I get back, but right now, I'm going to wake John up a little early so that I can give him a good work out also and a tasty suck that he'd never forget. Talk to you later."

"Okay, you little horny toad. Don't make John too, tired before he goes to work."

As soon as Virgil put the phone down, it rang again. She picked it up. "What do you want now, Liza?"

"Hi, honey, I didn't look like Liza the last time that I looked in the mirror," said the voice on the other end.

"Oh! Hi, baby, I thought that you were Liza again. You know how she's always calling and bugging me. When are you coming home Steve?"

"Well, to tell you the truth, I'm still in the Jamaica as we speak, but as soon as I finish up here, I have two weeks open before I have to be in Africa, so I'll be able to come home and see my most important ladies of my life.

Virgil, I miss you so much. You have no idea how lonely it is on the road without you and my daughter. I really appreciate you being so patient with me as I tour the world."

"Oohh! Honey, you know that I'll do anything that supports your career. I miss you too. I'm glad that you feel lonely without me, because that sister of mine sure does not.

She and her husband-to-be had the nerve to make out in the back seat while I was driving!" Virgil paused for a moment. "Steve, I have to admit I was pretty horny after that. So I guess it's hard for the both of us," she said softly.

Steve broke the silence. "Honey, can you do something for me?"

"Of course," she replied.

"Okay, good," he answered. "I want you to just relax and move your hand slowly down to your underwear and gently fondle yourself."

Virgil did as she was asked of, Steve, on the other hand, dropped his head back into the chair and imagined Virgil carrying out his task.

After a few moments passed in silence.

"How does it feel, Virgil? How does it feel to you? Is it wet?" Steve asked eagerly.

"Yes, honey, it's wet," Virgil replied, in such a low voice that it almost sounded like a whisper. Steve smiled and continued, I want you to close your eyes and picture me with my mouth wrapped around your pearl tongue.

Virgil let out a loud moan and began to move her fingers faster along with her hips as she headed for the hills of a climax. When all of a sudden, Virgil heard Steve say, "Okay, I'm coming."

"Are you coming, Steve?" Virgil asked between breaths.

"No, sweetie, I have to go back, or I'll miss my bus. They sent a runner to come and get me. Tell you what, cutie. We'll finish this later. I'll call you tonight."

"Okay, babe, I'll be waiting for your call," said Virgil sadly. "I love you."

"I love you too," said Steve.

As soon as Steve hung up the phone, he noticed a big lady wearing a short flowered dress staring in his direction. Steve placed a magazine over his erection as she walked over to him.

"That person that you were talking to on the phone musts be a special lady to make you rise like that," she said with a greedy gleam in her eyes. Steve was so surprised at her boldness that he was at a lost for words.

"That, uh, that was my wife I was talking to," he managed to say.

"Oh, okay! So where's your wife now?" she demanded to know as she placed her hands onto her wise hips.

'Wow, she is extremely curious and nosey,' Steve said to himself. "She's at home in another state." The big lady was about to speak, when Steve interrupted her.

"Listen, I would like to stand here and talk to you, but I have a bus to catch. So I'll have to see you later." Steve said as he turned and walked away.

Steve decided to take the short cut through the woods to reach the small village just a short distance away. He was only halfway through his journey when he saw the big lady again.

"I want to see the bulge that was inside of your pants earlier."

Steve was taken aback again by the boldness of this lady. 'This lady is something else,' he thought. "I'm sorry, Miss, whatever your name is, but I'm married and I do not have time for this!"

"So!" the big lady shouted. "You said so yourself that she was not here!" The big lady lowered her voice. "I can help you with your problem." She stepped closer to Steve and reached for his groin.

Steve jerked away. "Ohh! You want to play that way!" she said rubbing her hands across the top of her bubbly breast.

Steve took one last look at the big lady and started to run away fast. She caught up with him, tackled him to the ground, and landed on his back.

She forced her huge wide hands under Steve's body, found his most prized jewels, and begin to explore. Steve tried endlessly to stop the hard-on that was taking place, but, it seemed to have a mind of its own.

This made the big lady excited and full of herself.

"I knew that you wanted me," she said.

Steve wasn't amused. He dumped the big lady off of his back and tried to make another run for it. She grabbed one of his legs and threw herself on top of him. She pinned him down on his back and made her way up until she straddled his chest.

She ripped off a pair of flowered balloon underwear and tossed them to the side. They caught the wind and blew like a kite.

"I know that you want some of this Jamaican pussy," she bragged. She raised herself up just enough to slam her pussy on to Steve's face. "Eat it!" she ordered.

Steve could not breathe. The big lady's cum juices dripped all down the side of his face. 'I have to get this lady off of me,' he thought. He managed to raise his arms up and ripped her dress down the front.

The big lady was so pleased at this point that she almost hyperventilated. "Are you going to fuck me now?" she asked in a loud voice.

Steve nodded yes. "But, you will have to get off of me first," he explained. The big lady raised one of her large legs to get off of Steve, but quickly put it right back.

"How do I know that I can trust you?" she asked with a sarcastic rhythm with her head and neck. Steve ripped off the rest of the big lady's dress, grabbed both of her melons, and began to squeeze them.

The big lady moaned at Steve's touch. She slowly got off of him and laid on the soft ground of the dirt road. When she saw Steve begin to mount her, she closed her eyes, and just when she thought that he was going to give it to her. Steve jumped up and ran full speed to the village. The big lady got up quickly, yelling and screaming behind him. She stopped suddenly by the edge of the woods when she realized that she was not dressed appropriately enough to go into the village.

When Steve reached the point where the bus was to depart. Everyone was still breaking down and loading their equipment onto the bus. No one even noticed how dirty and bruised he was when he arrived.

Meanwhile, Virgil was at home, still lying on the bed. 'I can't wait until tonight. I need to release myself at this very moment,' she thought. Virgil begin to massage her clit and slowly slid four fingers inside of her wet tunnel.

When suddenly, the doorbell rang. "What is this? I can't even get busy with myself in peace around here," she said out loud as she fixed her clothes, and went stomping to the door.

Virgil opened the door with a jerk. "Oh, Mom, it's you," she said rubbing her eyes. "I wasn't expecting you until later on."

"Yes, I know. I was just on my way to the store to get some things for our trip to Lake Tahoe to meet your uncle Herman. Since he hasn't seen April yet, I was hoping that I could take her along with us. That is, if it's okay with you.

Your dad and I were thinking that you might need a break."

Virgil stood there for a minute in a moment of silence.

"I tell you what, dear, you just think on it a bit, and I'll go to the store. So call me later, okay? We're leaving in the morning so that should give you enough time to think about it."

Virgil quietly shut the door. She slowly walked to her room and sat on her favorite thinking place, her bed. 'She's right,' Virgil thought to herself.

'I do need to live a little and Steve probably wouldn't mind if April goes on a short vacation, just as long as she's back before he gets here.' Virgil quickly made up her mind she went into April's room and packed a huge black suitcase, making sure that April had everything that she needed for her trip.

Afterwards, she unplugged the phone and began to finish what she'd started before the doorbell ranged.

But, she ended up falling asleep instead.

It was four o'clock when Virgil finally decided to get out of bed. She plugged the phone back into the wall and it rang instantly.

"Hello, sleepy head, it's about time you got your lazy ass out of bed. What are you trying to do, sleep all day?"

"You know what, Liza? Just because you're on the rag doesn't mean that everyone else is."

"Very funny, Virgil, very funny. But anyway, I want you to come to Mom's house in about an hour, okay, Virgil?"

"No problem."

"I will be here," said Liza.

"What do you mean you'll be here? Do you mean that you will be there?"

"No, silly, I'm already at Mom's."

"Oh, okay then, I'll be there in an hour."

Hanging up the phone, Virgil decided that April might need a few more things, so she grabbed another suitcase and begin to fill it with more things just in case of an emergency.

As Virgil arrived in front of her parent's house, she saw her Mom and Liza getting into her mom's car. "Hey! Where are you guys going? Wait for me," she screamed and ran towards the car.

"Were you two trying to leave me by any chance?" asked Virgil, almost out of breath.

"No, we were only teasing you and you really didn't have to run and scream in the way that you did. The neighbors are staring at us so hurry up and get in," said Liza, trying not to laugh.

Looking around into the backseat, Virgil noticed that April wasn't in the car. "Mom, where's April?"

"She and your dad are taking a nap. So, did you make up your mind about what we discussed today?"

"Yes, I did. Her suitcases and things are in my car."

"I'm glad that you decided to let her go with us. You know she'll be in good hands."

"So where are we going today? Did you forget something else at the store?" asked Virgil.

"As a matter of fact, I did leave a few things, Virgil, and now I have to go all the way back to that damn shopping mall."

"Oh goody!" screamed Liza and Virgil at once, while giving each other high fives.

"Oh no," Mom broke in, "you guys are not going to have me in that shopping mall all day. We're going to stick together, get the few things that I came for, and when I get into the car, you had better be in it or you will be walking."

After her mom started driving off, Liza leaned over the seat and winked one eye at Virgil, letting her know not to pay any attention to what their mom said.

The following morning after their family left on their trip. Liza didn't waste any time convincing Virgil to go out again.

"Well, Virgil, what do you want to do tonight? You're a free woman. Your husband is gone, and your baby also left you. What is one to do with all of this free time?"

"I don't know, Liza, I guess it hasn't hit me quite yet."

"Oh, cheer up, girl. It'll be all right, just think of it like this: you have two whole weeks to yourself. Now what do we do with them?" Liza asked, as she put her arms around Virgil's shoulders.

"Well, I want to go somewhere that we don't hang out often, like that miniature golf place. Um . . . what's the name of that place? Um, it's right on the tip of my tongue . . . What is it?" Virgil struggled to remember.

"G-Balls," said Liza.

"Yes, that's it, Liza. What took you so long to rescue me from this agonizing headache that I was developing from trying to figure out that name?"

"Virgil! Why do you want to go and play golf? Golf is boring, and we don't know how to play the stupid game anyhow."

"Silly girl," said Virgil, as she whammed Liza hard with a pillow, "we're not going to play golf."

"Oh! Okay," said Liza, finally getting the picture finally.

At Gee-Balls, Liza and Virgil were just walking around and checking everything and everyone out, until Virgil spotted someone that she recognized.

She left Liza to go over to him. "Hi, Mike, remember me?"

"Of course," he replied. "My, have we changed," he said, checking out every inch of Virgil's thin body. "Has anyone told you how gorgeous you are?"

"No one so far," Virgil smiled as she took in the compliment. At that moment Liza walked over to them.

"So, Virgil, are you going to introduce me to your good-looking friend?"

"Oh, girl, I didn't even see you coming. You weren't trying to sneak up on me, were you?" "No," said Liza and she gave Virgil a push that almost knocked her over.

"Well, anyway, she continued, this is Mike. He and I go back a long way. And, Mike, this is my sister, Liza, who at this very moment has to leave. Don't you, Liza?"

"Yes, I do. I have to go and call John again because he's late. Catch you guys later," she said, rolling her eyes at Virgil as she walked away.

"Meet me back here around twelve or you'll turn into rags and walk around with one shoe on," Virgil yelled at Liza's back as she walked away. "Would you like to go for a walk, Mike?" Virgil asked.

"Sure, why not? We can go over to the running paths and do a little catch-up.

As they reached the park, Virgil noticed that there weren't many lights in that area.

"So, Mike, what have you been up to lately?"

"Well, not much."

"What do you mean by not much? That's not telling me anything."

"Do you remember when we used to date?" asked Mike, changing the subject.

"Yes, I do. What's that got to do with what you're been up to lately?"

"Well, as I recall, I never got a chance to kiss you."

"Of course you didn't, we were only in grade school."

"Well, we're not in grade school now."

"Does that mean that you want to kiss me, Michael Ross?"

Mike straddled Virgil while she sat on the park bench, putting his arms around her. He leaned forward and kissed her slowly at first. He tried to keep up with her way of kissing and when he got it, they engaged in a pool of lovemaking with their tongues.

Mike pulled away first, "Oh, Virgil," he said, with those same eyes that she had once seen with Kirk. "Virgil, I want you." He kissed her again, but this time, he took her hand and placed it on his cock. Virgil could feel the hard log underneath his loose fitting jeans.

"Unzip me, please. Unzip me," seemed to be what his zipper was telling her.

Virgil unzipped his jeans and reached inside the opening to get what she was looking for. Pulling back his underwear, Mike grabbed her wrist. "Let me lay on the ground first."

He removed his shirt she nibbled gently on his nipples and he moaned quietly on the grass. She moved up to his ears and flicked her tongue in and out of them.

Mike began to remove the rest of his clothes and stood up in front of Virgil, naked as the day that he was born.

'Oh my gosh,' said Virgil to herself as she removed her bra, letting her nice round breasts go free. They seemed to glow in the dim of the light. Mike immediately laid on top of Virgil with his hard groin pushing against her splashy clit.

His cock wasn't the longest or the thickest she's ever seen, but it was what was there, and right now, she wanted it.

Mike removed the rest of Virgil's clothes and they both rolled around on the grass a bit, just kissing and hugging and grinding without penetration contact. Until Mike couldn't take it any longer and gave Virgil one last roll to where he was on top of her, ramming his dick fiercely in and out of her twat. Before Virgil knew what had really happened, it was all over and Mike had come without her.

"I'm sorry, Virgil, I don't know why I did that."

"Is that all you can say? You barely lasted a minute. You were a waste of my time. I could have fucked myself longer than that," Virgil said, putting on her clothes as she stomped away.

"Wait! Wait, Virgil!" screamed Mike, tripping over his clothes as he ran behind her. "I'm sorry, Virgil, but I've been in jail. That is what I've been doing lately. It also is the explanation as to why I came so fast.

You're the only piece of ass that I've had in two years," he explained.

Virgil turned around when Mike caught up with her, she gave him a big hug, then kept walking without saying a word. "Call me," Mike said very sadly.

"Okay," said Virgil's without turning around.

Virgil walked a short distance around the golf park until she found Liza.

"You're here early, Virgil."

"So are you, Liza," Virgil said, still pissed.

"What's the matter with you, girl? Are you on the rag?"

"No. Worse than that. Cutie pie didn't size up. As a matter of fact, he lasted every bit of one eighth of a minute. He had me light a fire and he couldn't even put me out."

"Don't worry about it. I'm quite sure you'll find some way to put yourself out. Let's go home."

As soon as Liza and Virgil arrived at their parents house, John pulled up too. "You girls are slow. I dropped by G-Balls, but you must have left already, and you're just getting here."

"We stopped by Virgil's to get some clothes because she's spending the night with me tonight over here. I didn't know what time you were getting off, so I invited Virgil to spend the night to keep me company."

John put his head down. "Oh, you can come too baby," she said, walking up to him and giving him a big hug. "I wouldn't leave out my big bad teddy bear. Besides, there is plenty—enough room for all of us and more."

Virgil was still affected by her meeting with Mike. "Therefore, she did not hear a word that they said. "I just want to take a shower and start this day over in another time zone," she said out loud and walked away without saying another word.

Liza and John watched Virgil climb the stairs to her old room. They headed for the showers and retired also without saying a word.

Virgil knew that the morning had come, when she saw two people standing over her bed. She slowly opened her eyes and stared at them.

Liza yanked the covers off of Virgil. "Get up! Virgil, let's do something fun today." Virgil pulled the covers up over her head.

"Okay what?" Virgil asked, thinking that more sleep would be the fun that she had in mind.

"Well, I don't know about you guys," said John, jumping up and beginning to jog in place. "But I'm in for a little workout to tighten up some of these flabs, then I'll hit the outside Jacuzzi."

"That sounds good to us too," said Liza, pinching John on the tush.

Virgil thought that a workout would be an option to take her mind off of things, so she slowly got of bed. "Okay, then, it's final. I'll go and find something to wear. You two meet me back here and don't be upstairs doing the nasty either," she said, putting her hands on her hips.

When Virgil reached the Jacuzzi, she saw that John and Liza were already in it. They didn't even wait for her.

"What kept you, Virgil?" asked Liza.

"Oh, the phone ranged. It was Mom and Dad. They were just calling to tell me that April was okay. She asked what we were doing and to let us know that we only have one part-time maid and a butler to wait on us."

"Who needs them anyway?" Liza said, as she got out of the Jacuzzi.

"Where are you going, honey?" asked John.

"I'm done," said Liza.

"Well, so am I," said John as he hopped out, almost slipping as he struggled to catch up with Liza.

"You guys are weird," said Virgil, walking over to the exercise bike, and getting on it.

It must have been two hours since Virgil had heard a peep out of John and Liza, so she slowly walked over to the indoor Jacuzzi area. She peeked through the door just in time to see Ana, the maid, doing a Striptease show for John.

'I knew she's always wanted John, but she must be insane. Where's Liza?' Virgil wondered. She backed up and headed towards the kitchen. 'Maybe she's fixing something to eat.'

She approached the kitchen and stopped at the door. She put her ear to the door first because she thought she heard sounds. Peeking through the door, she saw that Liza wasn't in there alone.

She was bent over the counter with Douglas, (the butler) whose tongue was way up her ass hole. Virgil put her hands over her mouth. "Oh shit! What the hell is going on here?" said Virgil out loud.

Going back to the indoor Jacuzzi. Virgil wondered if she was going to look cautious or if she was going to be nice. She just burst open the door to the indoor Jacuzzi, but to her surprise, Ana was gone. John was sitting in the water without his trunks.

Liza came in from the kitchen.

"Hey, baby, it took you long enough to make those sandwiches."

"Well, I ran into Douglas and he kept rambling on about something that the yardman had done."

"Well, I'm not really hungry now, dear, so give it to Virgil."

"Yes, Liza, give them to me." Virgil took the food to the eating area, just on the other side of the open glass windows to the indoor Jacuzzi. And sat behind two beam poles.

She was only there a few minutes when through the open space, she saw John dancing around naked, with his cock slinging from side to side.

Liza got out of the water and started dancing with him against the wall. She got down on her knees and started sucking John's cock wildly. He was moaning loudly. He began fucking her mouth like a swollen pussy.

"Where do you want it, Liza? Where do you want me to shoot it? The hurricane is getting ready to erupt." Without removing his steam engine, she pointed to her mouth. John started to pump faster and harder, until his hot lava filled her throat and she swallowed it all.

"That's my girl," John said.

Feeling left out. Virgil ran upstairs to her room like a spoiled child and threw herself on the bed, wishing that Steve wasn't so far away. Then she got an idea. She opened her closet door and pulled out a huge dildo with life-like skin parts.

Moving over to one of the bigger mirrors on the wall, she removed her clothes, and posed for herself as she did a sexy dance with her long-lost friend.

Thinking about all of the things that she'd seen earlier, Virgil threw her head back, as she rubbed her big manless dick across her hard and hungry clit.

She purred like a cat and threw herself onto the bed, feeding her mouth with the manless dick in one hand and circling her clit with the other.

While her mouth was full with her play thing, she closed her eyes tight and imagined a naked stranger was watching her. Virgil had a very vivid imagination, which made the thought of someone watching her drive her wild.

She rolled over on to her stomach, wrapping her playmate into the blanket. Getting on top of it, she started riding it like a bucking bull. She could see herself on the closet door mirror, before closing her eyes again and keeping her imagination live.

She could see the stranger's rod come clearly. It was standing straight ahead now, like a tree limb. He motioned for her to keep her same position and move to the edge of the bed. The stranger started moving into a roundabout movement.

She backed up, and the stranger slid inside of her without missing a beat. He kept up that rhythm until his body shuttled like a stick shift out of gear. Virgil collapsed into a heap and the stranger disappeared.

Chapter 2

"Today's the day," Virgil said out loud to herself. "Today, Steve will be home. I'm so excited!" she kept saying to herself as she fed the dogs.

"I hope Steve isn't furious with me for letting April go on a little vacation, even though he hasn't seen his daughter in a long time.

Oh well, they'll be back way before he leaves. Besides, I'm in too good of a mod to let anything get me down today."

All of a sudden, Virgil paused to think about the times that Steve used to come home for lunch and give her a quickie, after he left, she'd jack off herself to be fully satisfied. 'If only he knew exactly how freaky she really was,' she thought.

It was half past eight when the doorbell ranged. "Steve!" Virgil screamed as she ran into his arms. "I missed you, Steve!"

"I missed you too, baby girl," he said, burying his face into her soft brown hair.

"Virgil, I want to introduce you to two of my new players and running buddies. Keair is my second hand producer from Jamaica and Salima is my first hand drummer from Africa. After a while, dear, I'll have a person from every country as a team player in my band."

They all laughed.

"I'm glad to meet you guys. I hope you would enjoy your stay. My Butler, Charles, will help you with your suitcases, show you to your rooms, and unpack your things if you want him to do so," said Virgil.

Keair smiled. "Oh, what a deal! Do you think you could fold them too because I was really in a hurry, so I just threw them in as is," Keair explained.

"Don't worry, Sir Keair, that's what I get paid for. You're not the first guest that's done that and you won't be the last."

Keair smiled again, slapped a fifty-dollar bill into Charles's pocket, wrapped his arm around his shoulder, and started blabbering on abut something as they walked upstairs.

That night Virgil cooked a nice Gumbo dinner, along with salad and sweet potato pie for dessert for Steve and his friends. "This is delicious, Virgil, did you make this yourself?"

"Yes, I did. I don't use the hired help all of the time. Sometimes I like to do things myself."

"Next time, Steve, we need to take your wife with us because her cooking makes me want to stay around her forever," said Salima.

"Why, thank you, Salima," Virgil said, blushing. "What about you, Keair? You haven't said a word since we started eating."

"Virgil, will you accept my deepest apology? I forgot to tell you that back in my country when we are around a big table and bundles of food is served, we are not allowed to speak until we are finished feasting.

But I'm finished now and I agree with Salima 100% percent."

"Virgil's big brown eyes widened with delight. So what do you think about it, honey?"

"We'll have to see about that. April is older now, so maybe, just maybe, I'll take you guys, next time, babe," he said, giving Virgil a big kiss. "I'll ask Mom when she comes back to see what she has to say about all of this," Steve laughed to himself.

After dinner, Steve and Virgil went for a midnight stroll through the woods behind their fenced-off estate.

"Virgil," said Steve pulling her close to him. "There's something I want you to do. I trust you, and I know that you have been a good girl. In order for us to keep our flame alive, (and may I add there's nothing wrong with it), we have to start doing new and exotic things to each other.

Because sometimes I can't take you with me. I don't want to drift apart from you, so we should try doing things that will keep us together always. You know, keep it interesting and exciting all the time even when we're apart. Giving us both a reason why we would want to see each other at all times. Are you following me so far?" asked Steve.

Virgil just gave him a puzzled look.

"Okay, honey, I think that I have to break it down to you so that you'll understand where I'm coming from. First of all, I think that we should start off by expressing our deepest fantasies to each other.

I think that we should be very open and honest to each other by telling one anther what sex means to us. Okay, for instance, if I ask you what do you want out of sex, what would you say?" asked Steve.

Virgil just stared at Steve with the most strangest look on her face. Reading Virgil's face, Steve stood up. "Virgil, I know this might be a little far-fetched to you, but I do love you and I don't have another woman.

I just want us to be together forever, and if we ever split apart, I want to remember you always. I hope you understand what I'm trying to say to you, honey."

Standing in front of him and focusing on a tree limb, Virgil said, "I understand what you are saying, Steve. I just want you to tell me what your fantasies are first since you brought it up."

"Okay, that's not a problem and I've been thinking about this for a very long time and I don't know any man who would give their wife this privilege." Steve paused for a moment.

"What I want is to watch while one or two men fuck you and after you're finished, I want to see how big your pussy look, it would really turn me on t fuck you afterwards while my dick drowns in your flowing river of cum."

Virgil opened her mouth wide in amazement. "Now I know it sounded a little blunt, baby, but there wasn't any other way to say it. That's one of my fantasies, honey, and that's the way I'm feeling right now because like I said before, if you're going to do it, I'd rather you do it in font of me instead of behind my back."

Virgil turned in another direction so Steve couldn't see the enthusiasm on her face. She was pleased to hear that Steve was as just as freaky as she was. "Okay, Virgil, it is your turn. Or, if you want, I'll give you a few days since I threw this on you without warning."

"No, no, that's quite all right, honey. I do have one and I better say it now, or I'll be afraid to say it later. I always wondered what it would be like to watch another man suck your dick." One of Steve's eyebrows went up he wasn't expecting that one.

"Why, honey, you have such a vivid imagination," Steve said, as he made room for her to sit down. "That probably would drive you into a triple orgasm. You want another guy to blow me," Steve said pointing to his mid section.

"Yes, dear, you wanted me to tell you my most erotic feelings. Don't you think it's okay?"

"Yes, it's okay, Virgil. That's fair enough. This conversation is going better than I thought. I was thinking that when I mentioned it you were going to beat me with a stick or something."

"Steve!" said Virgil, "I would never do that to you." as she grabbed his cheek and kissed it. "But, I'll think about it some more. It seems kind of strange for me to make love to someone else while you're watching."

"Okay, sweetie, I'll give you some time to think about it, then you can let me know on your own free will. Oh! One more thing, baby, if you decide to do it, you can't tell me when, where, or who it is. And that's the same for you. It's more exciting that way. Don't be afraid to answer me baby. I'm not trying to trick you or anything. I just want our marriage to be steamy, that's all. And don't get on the phone and call Liza to ask her advice, because she'll only confuse you." Virgil didn't hear a word he said because her mind was cluttered with questions about, what kind of guy it would it be? Is he sexy? Is he big? And how would it take place?

The next morning the sun beamed down on Virgil's face as she put the covers over her head and continued sleeping, trying to recuperate from the exercise that Steve had given her the night before.

She had a smile on her face as she thought about the things that Steve had said to her while they were making love. Until, Steve entered the room carrying breakfast on a tray.

"You missed breakfast, honey, so I had Rose to make you up a tray."

"Missed breakfast?" Virgil repeated. "How did I do that? I set the clock. Did you hear it go off?"

"Well, you were sleeping so good that I just didn't want to wake you, and I unplugged the phone."

"Why did you do that? I bet your friends think I'm some kind of old hag or something, and that I just sleep all day because I have hired help to do my work for me."

"Calm down, they understood. Besides, they weren't expecting me to make it either. So, did you think about what I asked you last night?"

"Gee, I don't know, Steve, we had a fifteen-minute walk back to the house, we took a shower together, made love all night, and here I am just waking up."

"I'm sorry," Steve said, giving her a little kiss. "I won't rush you again, unless, unless you take too long."

"Don't thank me, thank Rose. I just delivered it."

"Well, thank her for me," said Virgil with mouth full of food.

Virgil finally got out of bed an hour after she had finished eating breakfast. Staring into her closet, she couldn't seem to find anything to wear as usual. "Why do I have to go through this every time I want to get dressed?"

Why can't I find something and be satisfied?" Virgil said to herself.

"Talking to yourself again, girl?" asked the voice from behind her. Virgil turned around.

"Oh hi, Rose. Why do you always catch me talking to myself? Are you spying on me?"

"No, honey," said Rose with a laugh, "I didn't come in quietly, you would have heard me if you weren't so busy talking to yourself." They both laughed.

"Well, the reason why I came up is because Steve wants to know if you are getting ready to go sightseeing with him, Keair, and Salima."

Looking into her closet one more time, Virgil finally said, "tell him that I won't be attending. Tell him that I have a lot of thinking to do. He'll know what I'm talking about."

"Okay," said Rose, "I hope that you know what you're doing. I'll see you at lunch."

After Rose left, Virgil decided not to put on any clothes just yet. She just laid across the bed to do more thinking. She knew the answer, but now that it was getting close to the time to tell Steve, the more afraid she became.

She was hoping it was just a phase that she was going through, because she really wanted to do this. "I'll figure it out," she said aloud.

Virgil woke up the next morning with the feeling that she was being watched. She turned over to see Steve staring in her direction.

"It's okay, Steve."

"It's okay what?" asked Steve, pretending not to know what she was talking about.

"It's okay for us to live out our fantasies in front of each other."

Steve was so happy that he grabbed her and squeezed her so tight, that she let out a big scream. "Oh oh, did I hurt you, honey? I didn't mean to hurt you."

"It's okay, baby, really," said Virgil, trying her best not to show any pain. You have to remember that you go to the gym and I don't.

"I apologize again, baby. I'm just so happy that we understand each other on this. Not many couples can do this, so we can consider ourselves special. So when do we start?" asked Steve, waiting patiently for Virgil's answer.

"I don't know. I think we should come to some kind of agreement or something. You know, like rules and regulations." said Virgil.

"Honey! This is not a contract. This is our lives, okay?"

Let's just live it like we see it. Like I said, the only thing there is to remember is you don't have to know when it's going to happen. I tell you what, let's celebrate tonight, but it will have to be after nine.

I have to meet some people, some producers, at the airport. It shouldn't take no more than an hour or so. I'll try to get back as soon as I can get rid of them.

I'm taking Salima with me, because one of them is from his country, and they're going to have a night out on the town. Salima said to tell Rose not to worry about him because he won't be back until tomorrow evening.

But at about ten thirty, I want you to start some bubbles in the Roman tub, along with some champagne and open the shutter doors to the bathroom like we always do when we want to be romantic.

Light some candles, get some fruit and honey from the kitchen, and last but not least, don't forget that little red nightie that I brought you for Valentine's Day, the one that you never got to wear with the shoes, stockings, and the works."

Virgil was excited. "Wow! I'm in for a big night."

"You most certainly are, my little pumpkin," said Steve, kissing her on the cheek. As soon as Steve shut the door, Virgil raced to get everything together that Steve had asked her to do.

It took her two hours to find the stockings, which she was about to give up on, until she pulled the whole dresser drawer out and there they were. She pulled them out very carefully to make sure she didn't snag them on a splinter. After the stockings were found, Virgil took her time getting prepared for the big night. She plan the rest of the day carefully to make sure that everything was perfect.

When she finished.

The clock on the wall said ten. With only thirty minutes remaining, Virgil quickly finished up, removed her clothes, and climbed into the Roman tub with a sigh of relief. She was only in there a few minutes when there was a knock on the door.

"Come in," she said in a sexy voice, thinking that it was Steve. But, to her surprise, it was Keair, dressed in his bathrobe and slippers.

"What can I do for you this evening, Keair?" Virgil asked, in a very calm voice.

"I'm so sorry to bother you, Virgil, but I thought Steve would be hanging around here some place."

"No, I'm sorry, but he and Salima went out."

"Do you know where they went?"

"Yes, Steve was saying something about meeting some producers at the airport. He should have been back by now, it's taking longer than I expected."

"Oh," Keair said, reaching for the door.

"Keair," Virgil said, "could you wash my back for me?" Keair hesitated for a second. "Of course."

Keair picked up the washcloth and smoothen the suds around, and around up and down gently across Virgil's back. "I take it that you have done this before. You know just how to make a girl feel good."

Keair dropped the towel into the tub and picked Virgil up in one swoop and headed for the balcony with bubble-bath suds dripping down all parts of Virgil's tanned body.

Once on the balcony, Keair closed the balcony glass doors. It didn't take long before Virgil's hands were gripping the bar across the doors and her face was pressed firmly against the clean glass.

While Keair held her legs off the ground as he grind her full speed.

Steve watched with enjoyment. He could tell that Virgil was giving in to it. By the sounds of the purr's that she made when sex feels good to her. This made the hump in his pants feel really uncomfortable.

He put down the camera to free himself, but when he picked up the camera again, it was too late. Keair was standing over Virgil, releasing himself all over her face.

After Keair picked up his clothes and Left Virgil's room.

Virgil went into the bathroom to clean up, and as soon as she stuck one foot into the tub, Steve bent her over so far that she thought her head was going to touch her knees.

"That pussy looks juicy, baby—and wide. I want some now. I can't wait," said Steve, ripping off the rest of his clothes, and entered Virgil with a hard thrust.

"Virgil, Virgil, you just don't know how long I've waited for this," he said as he banged her at top speed. "Bend over some more, baby, this is feeling too good."

Virgil bent over some more, spreading her legs as wide as she could get them with one leg inside of the tub and the other one on the floor. "Honey, your pussy is really wet. I don't know if I'm going to be able to hold it."

"That's okay, honey, do the best that you can," said Virgil, trying to keep a good grip on the wall and the side of the tub, but her hands slipped, and she went down with a flop, but that didn't stop Steve.

He pushed Virgil up onto her knees and kept on pounding. Virgil's ass went into waves as Steve drilled away at her flooded cunt.

"Ooohh, Virgil, I'm feeling goose bumps. My dick is tickling! OOOHH! Virgil, I can't, I can't hold it any more . . . I'm . . . shit . . . I'm c-c-comm-ing." At that moment, Steve's body flushed with waves of pleasure, and Virgil was only seconds behind him.

They both collapsed on the floor. Virgil wiped the beads of perspiration from Steve's forehead. "Honey," said Virgil, in a low voice.

"Yes," Steve answered in the same low tone that Virgil just used. "How did you know that this was the time?"

"Well, Virgil, I had already set it up this morning because I knew that you were going to say yes."

"Oh really?" Virgil said watching him as he got upright to his feet. "Next time, I wish that you would warn me," said Virgil, wringing out her hair that was now drenched in sweat and water.

"Are you mad at me, Virgil? Because I sense some hostility in your voice. Sweetheart, I can't tell you when it's going to happen, because if I do, you'll feel uncomfortable and nervous. I don't want you to feel that way.

I want you to live for that moment without thinking about it, okay?"

"Okay," said Virgil, giving Steve a big hug.

"So tell me all about it," said Steve.

"What do you mean, didn't you see everything?"

"Yes, I did, but I want to hear it from the horse's mouth."

"Oh, okay. Well, it was different. It was like he had me in some kind of voodoo Jamaican trance. I felt like I was floating in the air. When he opened his robe and his manhood appeared.

I could have sworn that the damned thing told me to drop to my knees and suck it, and of course, I did just that."

Steve laughed.

"It's not funny," said Virgil hitting Steve across the head with a towel.

"It is too! I'm going to ask Rose if she put something in your tea. What is this talk about voodoo and his dick talking to you and things? Baby, you must go and lie down on the bed.

Because fucking two men in one night has really got your imagination running wild."

"Very funny, Steve. Very funny, we will see who's the crazy one when it is your turn," said Virgil.

The next morning at breakfast, Keair sat across from Virgil at the table. He looked at her and acted as if nothing happened.

In a way, Virgil was sort of offended, but then she thought. How was he supposed to act in a situation like this, especially, since I'm married to his best friend.

And to look on the bright side, she felt blessed enough in her eyes to be able to carry out her most wildest fantasies in front of her husband, she was having the time of her life, and it was her turn to plan the next experience.

Virgil did what she could to get through breakfast without making eye contact with Keair. She quickly ate her meal and turned to face Steve. "I won't be going with you guys today.

I have a few things to do before you leave this weekend. Is that okay with you, dear?"

"It's okay, baby."

Virgil kissed Steve fully on the lips. "Thank you for last night. Hon," said Virgil before she dashed up the stairs without excusing herself.

Once upstairs, Virgil looked through her old phone book for Phil's number. He was an old school mate that she grew up with.

Virgil paused for a moment with one hand on the phone and one finger by Phil's number. 'Now what should I say?' said Virgil to herself. 'Hello, Phil, I'd like to watch you suck my husband's dick. No, that's a little to forward.'

Virgil continued to think for a few more minutes. All of a sudden she jumped up. "I got it!" she screamed and dialed the number.

"It's ringing," she said in a low whispered.

"Hello," said the voice on the other end.

"Hello," said Virgil in her fake Jamaican accent that she'd picked up from Keair, just in case a woman answered the phone, or if she had the wrong number. "May I speak to Phil, please?"

"This is Phil. To whom am I speaking to?"

"This is Virgil."

"Virgil? This isn't the Virgil that was supposed to take her turn and call me back, is it? You know I've been waiting for months for you to call me, I thought maybe you'd decided to go on the road with your husband or something."

Virgil laughed. "I'm sorry that I never called you back. Here I am thinking that it was your turn when it was really mine. I tell you what, I'll make it up to you, that is the real reason for my call."

"You see," Virgil went on. "My husband and I are living out our deepest fantasies and we're allowed to watch each other have sexual encounters with other people. He has already gotten one in on me and now it's my turn to get one in on him.

Now what I'd like for you to do is to suck him off while I watch it happen. Do you follow me so far?"

"Yes, I'm right behind you, girl. Now let me get this straight, you want me to blow off your husband, while you watch. Uh, Virgil, does your husband know anything about this?"

"No, that's the whole idea. When one of us makes a plan, the other one is not to know what or when it's going to happen."

"Oh," said Phil, trying to create the picture inside his head. "One more question, Virgil. It doesn't make any difference to me whether he does or doesn't but do you think that Steve will blow me as well?"

"I don't know," said Virgil. "I don't think he's ever done this before, so for this time, I think we should stick to the basics."

"Don't worry, sucking off his cock to an erotic organism is plenty enough for me. So when is he leaving?" asked Phil.

"This weekend coming up."

Phil was very excited. "Okay, I will make reservations right now for Tuesday and I'll call you later with the details."

Virgil was also excited. "You won't regret this."

"I'll make sure that I don't," said Phil, laughing to himself. They both hung up at the same time. Virgil was so happy that she started making plans for the big day, along with her list that read:

(1) Pick Phil up from the airport. (2) Take him to a nice hotel and suite. (3) Tell Steve, that he is just an old friend from out of town. (4) Have him to invite us over for dinner. (5) Phil will accidentally spill some wine on Steve's pants, and Phil will just happen to have a pair that fits.

Virgil paused, then what? 'Old well, I'll think of something,' she thought.

Virgil was pretty nervous over the next few days, she was wondering whether Phil was going to make it or not and whether Steve was going to go through with the plan. She was also worried about being alone again when Steve left.

But all of those thoughts vanished when she imagined, Steve's steamy large dick, disappear deep down into Phil's hot throat.

With that thought, she grabbed one of her favorite books, from her private library shelf, labeled "SEX AND YOU." Flipping through the pages, she inhaled all the information that she could, about the thousands of ways that you can have sex, but her favorite parts of the book were the true based stories.

Virgil liked to seep deep into those stories using her upmost imagination.

Tuesday came very fast to Phil.

'It seems as if I just talked to Virgil yesterday. Phil thought to himself as he packed his things. I wonder what Virgil's husband is like?

I hope he goes for it. Oh well, if he doesn't, I'll still get a chance to see Virgil. I hope she didn't tell him that I was open to all sex, and if she did, I'll have to make him forget all about that. I'm very clean.

I get a checkup frequently throughout the year and if there are any diseases that are out there, I have plenty of doctor's results to prove that I don't have it.

Well, I hope that he likes me, and I better call Virgil right away to tell her that I'll be arriving at about four in the afternoon, giving us some sightseeing time.'

"Oh, look at me, I'm so nervous that my mind is occupied with continuous thoughts about Steve," said Phil giving one big final flop down on his suitcase to close it before he dashed to the airport.

Virgil arrived at the airport at about 4:05 p.m. she combed it for Phil's gate. Upon finding the gate, the area seemed to be deserted.

Virgil stood there for a minute, searching for the flight information in her purse, when she felt something in her hair.

She slapped at her hair without taking her eyes away from her purse. But when it happened again, she twirled around very quickly, looking right into the chest of none other than Phil himself.

"Phil! Gotdammit, I almost knocked you out. Do you always greet your long-lost friends this way?"

Phil chuckled. "Where's my hug?"

"Oh, sorry." Virgil gave Phil a hug. "Do you work out or something? Because I remember you as Phil the stick, not Phil the Body builder. Look at you! You're gorgeous. I can't help but touch your arms," she said poking away at Phil's biceps.

"Enough about me. You don't look too bad yourself, honey," said Phil, turning her around in a complete circle and pinching her ass.

"Okay, okay, before I seduce you right here in this airport . . . where do you want to go first?" asked Virgil.

"I think that we should go and get something to eat first because the food on the plane was horrible."

"Great, I could use some food myself. I know this great restaurant down the hill that sells the best southern food that money can buy. They have Southern fried chicken, home-baked bread, and red velvet cake, the works," she said as she counted the items with her fingers.

"Well, quit your babbling and hurry up and get us there, before I start eating you," he said. Phil and Virgil both faced each other and laughed.

After dinner, Phil wanted to change clothes and put on comfortable shoes before Virgil dragged him all over town. They made a quick stop at Phil's hotel suite and after thirty minutes had passed, Phil finally came out of the bathroom.

"I'm ready!" Phil was dressed in some purple jeans with the jacket to match. Virgil stared with her mouth wide-open.

"Where do you think you're going dressed so fine? Some woman is going to attack and rape you. You better watch out, boy."

"So do I really look that good?"

"Let's just put it like this, you look like my favorite dessert."

"Oooh," Phil said, blushing. "Don't get yourself into trouble, girl."

After leaving the hotel, Phil and Virgil covered a lot of ground—, from going to the movies, the zoo, roller skating, and ending it with a drink in a local bar.

Finally, at about five a.m., they finally decided to call it quits and turn in. Virgil slipped into her room without Steve's knowledge, at least that's what she thought.

As soon as she shut the door behind her she heard— . . .

"And where have you been, Mrs. Lady?" asked Steve, yelling directly into Virgil's ear, causing a ringing in that ear and scaring the shit out of her all at the same time.

Virgil jumped in fear. "Oh, I'm sorry, honey, I didn't mean to yell so—"

But his words were cut off by Virgil's fist beating against his naked chest. "Don't you ever do that to me again," Virgil screamed, picking up a small lamp and throwing it at him as he backed up.

Steve ducked, ran into the bathroom and locked the door to avoid physical harm, and the lamp spattered against the wall. Steve yelled from inside of the bathroom. "Honey, I'm sorry. It was a joke, don't you get it?

I didn't mean to yell so loud in your ear. Will you please try not to throw anything else at me? Look at it like this, we don't have much time left together. So we shouldn't spend the rest of it like this.

If I come out, will you promise not to hit me?" Steve continued to beg.

Virgil thought about it for a minute. "Okay, I promise."

"I'm coming out," Steve opened the door and slowly walked towards Virgil, holding out his hands.

"Friends," said Steve, laying down on the bed and pulling her down on top of him.

Steve rolled them over on their sides. "Now let's kiss and make up." Virgil untied Steve's pajamas. "You kiss, I'll make up." she said.

"Good, when you finish, will you go out and come back in again, so we can fight and make up once more?"

Without taking Steve's cock out of her mouth, and with her free hand, she playfully slammed a pillow onto his face.

"It was just a thought, that's why I'll hold it as long as I can, and you will be walking around tomorrow with lock jaw or something."

Virgil took her mouth off of Steve's cock, letting it bang sort of hard against his stomach.

"Okay, baby, just another one of my corny jokes. Just keep on sucking me into a wet orgasm, a deep sleep, and I'll see you in the morning."

"Well before you drop off to sleep, don't forget about our dinner date tomorrow. Make sure that you're home at about six, because we don't want to keep Phil waiting." said Virgil.

The next morning Virgil gave Steve another friendly reminder about their dinner date. "Remember, honey, put Phil on your agenda."

"Phil, . . . oh yes, I almost forgotten about him, but I will be on time. Also, Salima, Keair, and I have a late business lunch, I'll try not to eat too much. But, right now, we are going to play a little golf."

"Steve, now you know I do not like golf and I don't want to look stupid as I follow you guys all over the golf course."

"But, look at it like this, you will be my good luck charm."

Virgil put on her puppy dog face, but it didn't seem to work "Oh, honey, do I have to go? It's kind of boring when there's nothing for little old me to do."

"Is that your only concern? Well, you just don't worry your pretty little head because you can carry my rag that I clean my golf clubs off with."

Virgil gave him a weird look. "Fine! But, you owe me."

"I knew that I could convince you, baby. I'll see you downstairs in thirty minutes. Don't be late and dress comfortably." Steve rushed out of the room in a hurry before Virgil had a chance to change her mind.

Virgil got dressed slowly, as she bitched and complained to herself about going to the golf course, but the thought of having dinner later on with Phil put a smile back on her face.

Later on that day. Steve and Virgil arrived at Phil's hotel suite about ten minutes ahead of schedule.

After they knocked once on the door. Phil opened it and struck a pose for his guest, decked out with a black tuxedo, white shirt, and his favorite colored bow tie, purple of course.

"Do come in." Virgil and Steve entered the suite. "You must be Steve." Phil extended his hand and they engaged in a brief hand shake.

"I've heard so much about you within the last few days. This lady next to me has spoken highly of you. And by the way, this is my wife, Virgil." Everyone laughed.

"Just a little humor to get the evening started," said Steve.

Phil noticed that Steve also had on a tux. "I see we have something in common," he said pointing at Steve's tux.

"Oh yes, someone said that I would be over dressed if I wore this, but I will not call out anyone's name." said Steve, glancing into Virgil's direction as he said it. Virgil put her head down and gave a little shy grin.

"Phil, you didn't tell me that you were wearing a tuxedo." said Virgil.

"I didn't know either, but for some reason, this seems like the only outfit suitable for this occasion. In other words, this is the only appropriate suit that I have with me. I was in such a rush to get here that I almost forgot the damn thing on my bed."

"That's okay, Phil, I think you look nice in it, almost good enough to eat," Virgil said, winking at Phil as she thought about a joke that she and Phil shared just the day before. Phil also blushed with the same thought in mind as Virgil.

"You two guys have a seat," said Phil as he motion for them to sit down on the nice sofa. The waiter will be here shortly to serve us drinks. Meanwhile, I will go and freshen up if you will excuse me please."

Before Phil left, he clapped his hands so that the waiter would serve the drinks while he was out of the room.

After dinner, they were served some delicious pecan pie.

"This pie is divine." "I'll have just one more piece," said Virgil as she cleaned her plate.

Steve laughed under his breath. "Oh, I don't know, Virgil, you don't want to ruin that perfect figure of yours."

Virgil cut the pie and placed a slice on her plate. "Don't worry, honey, I'm quite sure you will find some kind of activity to help me get rid of it."

Steve laughed, wildly, knocking his wine right onto his lap and all over his nice white shirt as Virgil and Phil had planned.

Virgil wasn't concerned about cleaning Steve's shirt as she moved slowly to dry it. Steve placed his hand on top of Virgil's. "That's fine, honey, I don't think that it is coming out. I'll just have to take it to the cleaners tomorrow."

"But I'm . . .—"

Steve cut her off. "Don't worry about it, honey, it's not one of my better shirts, I'll just go and buy a new one."

Phil, whom was quiet during the whole ordeal, broke in and said. "Steve, if you wouldn't mind, I have an extra shirt. We're about the same size, so it should fit you just right."

"The shirt is not what I'm worried about, it's the pants," explained Steve. I also have a pair of extra trousers to fit you also. You can try them if you like," offered Phil.

"Why, thank you, Phil. That's very generous of you. I think I'll do just that before my clothes begin to stick to me. Lead the way. Honey, I'll be right back." Steve got out of his chair and followed Phil.

"Boy, this is a nice suite you got here, Phil," said Steve. While he looked around the bedroom.

"Yes, I know. I was surprised myself when I first saw it. Phil answered Steve without taking his eyes away from his suitcase as he looked slowly to find Steve something to wear. "Here we are, I was beginning to worry there for a moment.

I thought that I'd left these pants behind along with some other things that I forgot to bring. They're just a tad bit wrinkled, but they're not wet," laughed Phil.

Steve unzipped his own pants and let them drop around his ankles. Phil turned into the other direction to avoid starring. Steve put on Phil's pants and was having a problem zipping them up.

"Phil, I think this zipper is stuck or something. Could you just help me with this if you don't mind."

"Yes, just as I planned," Phil said to himself as he turned and walked towards Steve. "What seems to be the problem?"

Steve jerked on the zipper to demonstrate to Phil. "I can't seem to get it to go up."

"Here, let me try. Maybe I can get it up for you." Phil begin to get a chill down his spine as he took the zipper in hand and begin to pull on it. Meanwhile, Virgil crept inside of the room's closet, watching and waiting for something to happen.

After several attempts to resolve Steve's little problem. Phil decided that it would be a good idea to get down on one knee and try to fix the zipper from the inside, brushing against Steve's cock on purpose. "I'm sorry," said Phil, trying not to get too excited.

Again, Phil tried the zipper, but this time, he used his teeth and expelled air from his nostrils to breathe hard enough so that his airway would move the hair on Steve's legs.

Steve was trying desperately not to allow an erection to emerge but, by blowing on his leg hairs was one of Steve's weakest points.

Phil noticed that Steve's chest was rising and falling a little higher than usual, so he thought that he'd make another move by rubbing the back of his hand slowly across Steve's dick.

Steve jumped back a little, but didn't say a word. He took a deep breath and stepped back up to his original spot.

"I tell you what, Steve, I need you to take off these pants and I'll see if I can fix them another way." You can sit on the bed. This will only take a minute.

After sitting on the bed for several minutes, Steve came to the conclusion that Virgil had set this up. He went into the room where they ate dinner, but she wasn't at the table. He looked on the balcony and she wasn't there either, but he knew that she was close by.

He then turned around and bumped heads with Phil, to whom was showing a very large bulge in his right pants pocket.

"I don't know about this," said Steve to himself as he held his hands up to his forehead in an effort to remove the pain from his head.

"You can lay down on the bed. You'll feel more comfortable. I didn't mean to bump into you so hard."

"No, I'm fine. I think I'll just change back into my other clothes and go home." Steve grabbed the pants that he had on when he arrived, and sat on the bed to put them on, before he realized what was going on, he was pushed back and Phil's mouth was snugged tightly around his dick.

He wanted to pull away, but the sensation was one that he'd never experienced before in his life time. Steve soon found himself massaging Phil's hair and feeling sort of relaxed as Phil sucked his toes into a curl.

Phil was sucking wildly, causing pre-cum to flow from Steve's erected cock.

"Oh shit, SUCK MY DICK! and don't forget about the balls!" Yelled Steve as he closed his eyes, forgetting about where he was and to whom was really sucking his dick.

Phil got so excited that he pulled out his long hot rod and began to masturbate with his free hand. Meanwhile, Virgil, was inside of the closet with her panties off and her legs gapped wide as they rested on Phil's suitcase.

Virgil didn't seem to mind fingering away at her big juicy cunt. Streams of thick rich cum had already made a path down her inner thighs.

Suddenly she heard that noise that she had been longing to hear, the beautiful sound of two people coming together and at the same time. That pleased her to see her husband and her best friend collapsed into the same ecstasy.

Virgil silently tipped-toed out of the closet and laid on the hotel suite sofa. She was still half-naked and alone, but her mission was accomplished. She laid on her back, with thoughts about what just occurred.

She quietly picked up where she'd left off inside of the closet, bringing herself to an earthquake of an orgasm, and sweeping away into a deep sleep. She was a happy woman.

The next morning, Virgil and Steve said their good-byes to Phil, and Virgil gave him an extra special thanks for helping her out with the fantasy with Steve, by slipping a reimbursement check for his flight ticket and hotel fee in his suitcase without him knowing about it.

On the way home, Virgil and Steve were very quiet, no one said anything. Steve didn't speak until they got into the privacy of their own bedroom.

"Aren't you going to say anything?" he asked, pulling off his clothes to take a shower.

"What are you talking about?" said Virgil, dashing into the bathroom ahead of Steve to get into the shower first.

Steve hopped in the shower behind her. "Don't pretend that you don't know. You probably were in the closet somewhere, peeking in on us like a little mouse."

Virgil's mouth dropped opened. "How did you know that I was in the closet?"

"So you do know what I'm talking about! You were inside of the closet peeking."

"Yes, I was in the closet and I'll admit that I enjoyed every minute of it."

"I never thought that I'd ever do that, you really surprised me. When I finally realized that I've been had by you, I didn't think that I'd enjoy it. I thought that I'd go home and scrub myself like a victim, but when he wrapped his tongue around my rod."

Steve pointed to his dick. "I couldn't stop the feelings. The funny thing is, I really thought that I was in there to change my pants and that's it. I never suspected a thing until he started fixing my zipper and brushing up against me.

You know, I think that that zipper was already broken. I'm glad that we can understand each other," said Steve, pulling Virgil closer to him and giving her a big hug.

"Now let me show you what Phil taught me." Steve dropped to his knees and wrapped his tongue around Virgil's dripping wet clit.

Chapter 3

Virgil was awakened by the sound of a baby's cry. Jumping up out of bed and almost tripping over her long pajamas, she ran into April's room to find Steve taking off her soaking wet diaper and getting her ready for a bath.

"April! When did she . . . ? Why didn't you wake m?"

"Calm down, honey. Your mom and dad brought her this morning because they didn't know whether they'd missed me or not, and I didn't want to wake you. Now she's just a little hungry and wet, that's why she's crying.

Just because I haven't seen her in a while doesn't mean that I don't know how to take care of my own daughter."

"Sorry, I'm just glad that my baby is at home." Virgil picked April up and raised her high up in the air so that she could get a real good look at her and then squeezed her with a big hug.

"Okay, Okay, that is enough. This is father—and—daughter hour, so you go downstairs and get her a bottle I'll take care of everything up here." And when you come back, we'll take April out into the world. It is a nice day today."

After going shopping and having a picnic in the park, April was a very tired camper. Virgil carried April to her room while Steve watched from the door.

After laying her down for a nap, Virgil walked over to Steve's side and they both watched April as she slept peacefully inside her crib.

"We have such a beautiful baby," said Steve.

Virgil pulled Steve over to the rocking chair, urged him to sit and she sat on his lap. "Yes, we do," she said.

"She has grown so much since the last time that I saw her and it's so hard to believe that I'm leaving her again. Before long, she'll be walking, talking, and I'll miss it all.

But you know, I've been thinking about taking a vacation after this tour and do concerts only close to home so that I can be near the two most beautiful women in my life. I don't want her to forget me. I want to be there for her, while she is growing up."

Virgil quickly turned to face Steve. "Do you really mean it? When did this come about?"

"When I held her again, and right now as I watch her sleep. I've thought about it for a long time, but I kept putting it off and putting it off, until today when I was getting April out of the tub. She raised her little hand up and touched one side of my cheek, looked into my face and smiled.

I then knew that I had to take a rest and spend some quality time with my family."

"Before you leave, we should bring out the video camera and have Rose make a family movie of us when April awakes from her nap." Virgil suggested, feeling god about Steve's decision.

"I love you, Steve. I'm glad that you are going to be spending more time with April and I, I dreamed that this day would come, but I wasn't expecting it so soon.

Do you think that when you are home and we are around each other that we'll argue, fight, and disagree all the time?" asked Virgil.

"I can't promise you that we won't, baby, but I can promise you that my love for you is forever. We have an understanding that's beyond anyone's belief.

Our love is so powerful in a sense that it scares me sometimes, but we can't let society ruin our love with their definitions of what a marriage should be all about. And to them, what we do is insane.

They figure that we are some kind of freaks or something, with their little insults for example: How could you let your husband do this, or how could you let your wife do that? So please, Virgil, don't let it affect the way that we feel about each other.

So let's make it official now, that we won't be victims of society," said Steve.

"You're right, Steve. I don't know how I can let someone come between the fantasies of our love. It seems that since we started this thing, our love making has improved one hundred percent.

"Don't worry, Steve, I won't let them get to us because we have it better than that."

"I just had a thought, Virgil. Steve reached over and squeezed her left tit. I'm leaving in about twelve hours. I have a fantasy of my own to show you, and you can watch if you like."

"Why can't you just tell me about it?" Virgil asked, removing his hand.

"Because I can show you better than I can tell you," said Steve, putting his hand back.

"What if I don't want to hear it?" said Virgil as she got off of Steve's lap and walked into the hall.

Steve sat in the chair a moment, watching her walk away before he dashed up behind her, slipping his hands under her skirt and pulling back her panties in the front so that her clit was free to fondle without interruptions.

"And what are you doing, sir?" asked Virgil with sarcasm in her voice, but a smile on her face.

Steve answered her in a deep voice, "I'm trying to seduce you, my fair lady."

Virgil slipped her hands down into Steve's shorts. "Why sir, what big dick do you have. I'm not sure that I'll be able to handle such a big tool as yours."

"I will be gentle," said Steve in that same deep voice as he picked her up, over his shoulders and pushed her into the hall closet.

"Steve, what are you doing? What if someone sees us?"

"No one will see us, babe. Besides, I've never done it in a closet before."

"You could have at least chosen a walk-in closet instead of this Cracker Jack box."

"Don't worry about it, babe, this is perfect. Now I'm going to reach up there and wrap my arms around that hanger rod while you put my legs over your shoulders and suck me until I can't hang anymore.

Get it, babe? Until I can't hang? It was a joke, Virgil, you we're supposed to laugh."

"Well, Steve, it was so funny that I forgot to laugh."

"Well, next time—, ooohh, that's n-ott fairr, V-i-rg-i-l, I was—n't fin—ished saying—Oohhh shit—my peace." Steve words were interrupted as Virgil licked the tender bare spots between Steve's balls and his upper thighs.

"Who said this was fair?" said Virgil before she put Steve's whole cock into her mouth.

"That's okay, honey. Don't you worry, sweetheart, pay back is a mother, . . . When you get finished, I'll do you a favor and fuck you senseless."

Later on that night while Virgil and Steve lay into each other's arms . . .

"I think that you shouldn't wake me when you leave."

"Why not?" asked Steve.

"Because you know how I hate to tell you goodbye. I try to hide the tears when you leave, but they always get to me anyway. So I was thinking if we try something different, then it probably won't hurt so much."

"Are you sure you want to do it that way?"

"Yes, I'm sure." With no other words to say, they closed their eyes to fall asleep.

At day break, Virgil rolled over and felt a body next to hers. Her heart stopped, thinking that Steve missed his plane. She was almost afraid when she looked.

'What the hell,' she thought, while jerking back the covers.

"Liza! Liza! Get up." Virgil screamed, slapping her sister on the head.

"What! What! What!" Liza asked, raising up to face Virgil.

"When did you arrive?"

"Last night, dammit. I've been trying to get a hold of you, but you're a very busy lady."

"What the hell have you been up too? I figured if I got in bed with you as soon as Steve jumped out, then you can't get away again."

Virgil laughed. "Are you kidding? I could have laid April down kicking and screaming and you wouldn't have known."

"Well, I was tired and I still am." said Liza.

"What time did Steve leave?"

"Well, John and I got here about two o'clock. We didn't know that he was still here. The next thing that I knew he was saying goodbye to everyone.

Rose made plenty of food for them to take on their trip so you don't have to worry about him eating."

"So how was your trip?" asked Virgil, changing the subject.

"Oh, girl, it was something else. John and I had the nicest time."

"By the way, where is he?"

"Well, he and I stayed longer after his business was taken care of. Before we knew it, our time was up and we ended up back here."

"So let me get this straight, your honey is at work like always, and mine is gone out of the country again. We have all of the luck, don't we?"

Liza pointed to the clock. "And it's five o'clock in the morning, so what should we do?"

Virgil smoothed the sheets out and made herself very comfortable. "Oh, that's a good one. Let's play Simon Says."

Liza agreed. "Okay." Not knowing what to expect.

Virgil turned her back to Liza to get even more comfortable. "Simon says go to sleep."

Liza laughed to herself and followed the command.

Chapter 4

Liza pressed her nose hard against the glass as she looked out of the upstairs window. Let's put on our jogging suits and go for a nice jog around some blocks.

"You! asked Virgil? Want to go jogging? The laziest woman in all of the world. There must be something interesting out there to make you come up with such an idea on your own.

The only way that I can make you work up a sweat, is when it's benefiting Liza. Now move out of the way so I can see why you're making your face print on the glass." Virgil looked down out of the window.

"Well, well, well," she said, pushing Liza aside. "Is that what you were looking at?" Virgil pointed to a guy across the street, sitting on a bench, putting on some shoes and appearing to be getting ready for a jog.

He looked very tall when he stood up, had a thin face, a beautiful tan, nice legs, and a cock that bulged in the front that was breathtaking to her. Virgil moved herself away from the window and walked towards the bathroom.

"Okay, last one in the bathroom to get dressed is an rotten egg," and she closed the door.

Liza rushed in behind her. "You're sure in a hurry." said Liza, trying her best to get dress before Virgil.

Virgil walked out of the bathroom again to exchange jogging suit. Liza walked behind her. "Quit your blabbering," said Virgil. Hurry up and get dressed before he leaves us." Virgil went back into the bathroom slamming the door behind her.

Liza opened the door almost as soon as Virgil shut it. "So what are we going to do, follow him all over the neighborhood?"

Virgil slowly turned Liza around by the shoulders, "You know, Liza, sometimes you talk too much. Now go get dressed."

Virgil and Liza finally made it outside and looked up and down the block for the unknown jogger.

"Okay, Virgil, since you're the expert, maybe you can tell us where the beef went."

"He's quick, I know that he couldn't have gone too far away that fast," said Liza.

The park is five blocks away, maybe he went there." said Virgil.

"Five blocks!" "Virgil, are you crazy? These are not like the regular blocks, these blocks stretch, and you know I'm not into this jogging shit."

"Liza, quit your whining and come on."

"And what if he's not there?"

"Then we'll catch the bus back."

"I can live with that." Liza smiled and took off jogging first.

Virgil and Liza had only been running for a short period of time when Virgil spotted the jogger.

She pointed her long finger in the jogger's direction. "Is that him over there?

"Yes, it is," replied Liza. "We found him and he's sitting down. Let's go take a seat on each side of him and rest."

Upon reaching the jogger Liza was the first to flop down on one side of him.

"Hi, my name is Liza. This is my sister and best friend, Virgil."

"Virgil, that's a very pretty name," said the jogger.

Virgil stared into the jogger's eyes. "Why, thank you."

Liza gave the jogger a pat on his upper thigh. "What's your name?"

"My name is Larry."

"It's nice to meet you, Larry." Larry took Liza's right hand and kissed it.

Virgil extended her hand to him. "Me too, I want you to kiss my hand too.

Larry kissed Virgil's right hand also, some awkward moments past and Liza was the first to speak.

She put her hand on Larry's thigh. "So, Larry, how often do you jog in the park?"

"Oh, about three times a week. I'm here in town because, of my grandparents. They don't get around like they used to and since I'm the nearest relative. It's my turn to take care of them for the next six months.

When my cousin comes home from his tour overseas, then he'll take over. But until then, I'm here to take responsibility for the fort."

Liza gave Larry's leg a tender grip. "That is so sweet, Larry. You seems to be a very nice guy. Are you seeing anyone at the moment?"

"Well, since I made it into town last month, I've only met one girl. Well, at least I thought it was a girl. She was very beautiful and had a nice slender body, nice feet, and long pretty braids in her hair. We went to a movie, and she invited me to her house.

I thought that I was going to score. She put on some music and we danced really close, and I didn't feel anything. You know, with us being so close together and all. She pulled away and said she'd be back.

She had to go to the little girls' room. The music was kind of loud and I wanted to be careful so I followed her to the bathroom unnoticed, and you know how it sounds when a man takes a whiz."

Liza and Virgil shook their heads, knowing what he was going to say next.

"I wanted to make sure, the door was slightly ajar, and that's when I saw it. Boy, did I get out of there quick."

"Oh my gosh!" I would have liked to have seen the look on your face!" exclaimed Liza, trying to picture it all inside of her head.

Virgil let out a giggle. "So I guess you haven't dated since."

"No, after that happened, you can never be too careful."

"Well, don't worry, Larry. Virgil and I are real women, do you want to see?"

"Liza!" "You'll have to excuse my sister. Her brain loves to put in extra innings."

Larry laughed, "You guys get along pretty good to be sisters. I know some sisters that wouldn't be caught dead together, but you two are different."

Liza gave Virgil the old wicked eye. "We know. Everyone is always telling us that."

Liza's hand is now higher on Larry's thigh. "What are you doing tonight?"

Larry thought for a few. "Just, the usual, I'll make sure my grandparents take their medicines before they go to bed, then read, draw, . . . stuff like that."

Liza frowned. "Sounds boring."

"No, it gets pretty exciting, especially when you try to tell two people that are much older than you to take their medicine before they go to bed, you get lots of static. Believe me, it's much harder than it seems.

After the fighting, I go to my room and do a little drawing and sometimes I let the T.V. watch me.

Larry was saying all the things that Liza wanted to hear. "I didn't know that you can draw."

"Yeah, that's what I do for a living. I'm an architect, but for the moment, I'm on a long vacation from big jobs. Starting Monday, I'm doing a favor for a friend. He needs me to do some comic strips for him. He called me as soon as I got settled.

I didn't want to take it, but it will give me something to do while I'm here."

"Well, if you're not too busy tonight, Virgil and I would like to see some of your drawings."

"Why, sure! Sure you can, I could used the company. Is that okay with you, Virgil?"

"Yes, we will be there." Virgil said slowly. 'I hope she hasn't forgotten about John,' Virgil thought, as she watched Larry get up and begin to walk away.

As soon as Larry was completely out of sight, Liza said. "Ouch! Virgil! Why did you pluck me on the ear?" "Because, you've forgotten about the big dinner that you and John are supposed to be having tonight?"

"Ah shit!" "What are we going to do? He has the whole night off too. We have to think of something."

"What do you mean by we?"

"Well, you know, you and me, we always stick together."

"Oh no," said Virgil, backing away. "You are not going to get me in the middle of this one."

"Oh, come on, Virgil. I'll talk Larry into painting us in the nude while he's wearing skin tight biker shorts and a torn sexy tank top. Now think about what you could imagine while you're sitting there with no clothes on.

He's standing across from you with a big knot in his shorts. So what do you say?"

Virgil put one finger on her cheek and looked into the sky as if to put the whole situation into perspective. "I guess that sounds pretty fair."

"I'm glad that you're with me on this one, Virgil, because I would've hated to go by myself.

Virgil started to say something to Liza, but changed her mind. 'I'm going to leave that one alone,' she thought.

Half way home, Virgil couldn't stop thinking about what Liza said. This made her very excited and she couldn't wait until the moment came.

When she made it home she headed upstairs to dissect her closet to find an outfit.

While Virgil was searching for something to wear, Rose entered the room with the house phone. "It's for you, Mrs. Virgil."

"Hello?" said Virgil.

"Virgil, this is John. Have you by any chance seen Liza today?"

"Yes, she's in the shower. Is there something that you want me to tell her?"

"Yes, I just wanted her to know that we'll have to put our dinner on hold. Something came up. Tell her I don't know exactly what location that I'll be working at, but I'll call her as soon as I get to the office and find out.

If you guys would stay there for a little bit, I'll get that information right away and get right back to you."

"We were going out for a little while, but I'll make sure that we stay here for your call."

"If for some reason that I don't get right back in touch with your guys, I'll try and call you again later on. Thanks, Virgil. Bye," said John. They both hung up the phone.

Just then Liza came out of the bathroom. "Who was that on the phone?"

"John," replied Virgil. "He called to cancel dinner. Something came up again, a meeting or something."

Liza quietly clapped her hands and jumped up and down. "In that case, I don't have to make up a lie."

Virgil looked at Liza and shook her head slowly. "Stop that and get dressed we have to leave." Liza laughed and obeyed Virgil's command.

Meanwhile, Larry was spending an hour straightened up his room to please his invited guests, that he was expected to arrive at anytime.

He put flowers on the desk, potpourri in a shiny crystal bowl which sat on the window sill, and for a finishing touch, he put in one of his favorite jazz CDs to help everyone relax.

He stood in the doorway to take a quick view of the room, "Perfect," he said to himself.

"I don't think that it's enough."

Larry turned around quickly. "How did? How did you guys get in?"

"Your grandfather let us in on his way out to walk with your grandmother down the street to play bridge." Liza said.

"My grandma play bridge on Monday and Thursday nights. Can I offer you two a drink?" he asked as he eyed Liza's nice breast, through her tightly fitted see-through blouse.

Virgil raised her hand. "I'll have a glass of wine if you have it."

"And I'll have the same," said Liza, giving Larry the same eye that he gave her as he left to go get their drinks.

Virgil took a good look around Larry's room. "This is a very big room."

Liza nodded in agreement. Larry returned moments later with their drinks.

A minute or two passed before anyone said a word.

"Oh yes, Larry finally spoke, I almost forgot, let me show you some pictures of my drawings." He pulled out a drawing of his after going into his file cabinet and babbling on about how he got started in his field of work. Liza didn't hear him of course; she was too busy starring at the front of his pants.

"As a matter of fact," Larry continued to blabber on, "I used to do nude sittings."

And that was the only thing that Liza heard. "Nude sittings?" she repeated.

"Why, yes, is there something wrong with that?"

"Why, no, no, there's nothing wrong with it. I'm just a little well . . . ," said Liza, calming down, "I didn't think . . . think that you were interested in . . . ." she paused.

"It's okay, I know what you're trying to say" Larry let out a low toned laugh. "Don't worry, you can talk to me freely about it. I don't mind."

"Okay," said Liza, feeling more relaxed now. "Did you have fantasies about the people that you painted?"

"Sometimes I did, if it was a woman."

"Oh really?" Liza moved a little closer to him. "Tell me all about it."

"Well, one day I decided I was going to stay after class. I followed the model that I'd just painted unseen to her dressing room, and there is where I found her down on both knees, giving this great big, huge guy a blow job.

I didn't know whether he was her boyfriend or not, but he was just too big for me to fight. After that, I was too ashamed to go back."

"If it would make you feel better, I'll let you paint me in the nude."

"Are you sure Liza?"

Liza had a sex hungry gleam in her eyes. "Sure! It will only take me a sec to get ready." Liza walked halfway to the bathroom and turned around. "Oh! I almost forgot. Can I borrow a robe or something?"

"You sure can." "There's one hanging on the door."

"Thanks." she said blinking one eye at Virgil. A few minutes later, the door to the bathroom opened and Liza stood in the entrance.

She, walked slowly out of the bathroom while modeling for Larry and Virgil. "How do I look?"

"Well, we don't know yet." "You still have on the robe."

"Ha-, ha-, ha, very funny, sis. I'm not taking it off yet."

Larry was all eyes. "You look great."

"Why, thank you, at least someone in this room knows good taste when they see it." Liza sat down on a flat table in the middle of the floor. "Is this fine?"

"That's fine, Liza." Larry begin to separate his paints to get them ready for the perfect colors. He looked up for a moment at Liza and then back to mixing his paint.

"I need you to do one little, tiny thing."

"What's that?" asked Liza.

"I need you to lower the robe and only expose the parts that you want me to paint."

Liza slowly got up off the table and let the robe drop to her feet. Larry took a hard swallow.

He stuttered when he spoke. "So . . . so that's what you want me to paint." His heart skipped a beat when he saw the beauty of Liza's straight hard nipples, the ebony color of her skin, and most of all, her almost hairless cunt.

The sight of all of this was almost too much for him.

'Can I really go through with this? Larry thought. I haven't started painting yet, and my dick is already on hard. Lucky for the paint smock, or I might scare them away.'

"How do you want me to pose?"

"Uh?" was all Larry managed to say, as he tried to snap out of his thoughts.

Liza repeated herself. "How do you want me to pose? Are you okay?"

"Yes, I'm fine. I was just . . . uh . . . I was just trying to think of the right paints to use." Larry, pretended to look for some paints in another drawer. "Oh well, I guess I can't find them. Regarding your question, Liza, whatever makes you comfortable."

"In that case." Liza opened her legs, showing her nice long pink—and—brown pearl tongue. I'll just pose like this."

"Okay, that's good. Now, what are you going to do with your hands?"

Liza positioned both hands on her breast.

"Okay, that's great." Larry, was feeling more intense now than before. "You can rest for a moment, Liza, while I go and get some water."

After Larry left Liza whispered to Virgil from across the room. "Virgil, I have a plan. Let us both ball him. When I give you the wink, you start doing your thing. So what do you think?"

"Why not? Because if I look at any more of these naked pictures, I'm going to need to attack somebody."

"Sounds like a plan to me."

"Here he comes," whispered Virgil, sticking her head back into the book as if nothing happened.

Larry came back into the room and positioned himself on his drawing stool. "Sorry for the delay."

"Oh, that's okay. Let's do this," said Liza, getting back into her position. As soon as Larry begin to paint, Liza blinked at Virgil. Virgil then unbuttoned the top part of her blouse. Larry was so deep into painting Liza that he didn't notice Virgil.

So Virgil took the pictures over to the bed and laid down across the bed with her skirt revealing a small portion of her soft, round butt cheeks. She was still failing to get Larry's attention, so she dropped some of the pictures onto the floor as a last result.

Larry quickly turned his head in Virgil's direction. Liza didn't move a muscle.

"I'm sorry." Virgil bent down to pick the pictures up, letting her breasts fall forward through her unbuttoned blouse.

"Do you need any help, Virgil?" asked Larry feasting his eyes on Virgil's rounded tits.

"No, thanks. I've got it." Virgil was relieved now that she'd finally gotten his attention. Larry continued to paint Liza but he was having a difficult time doing it.

'He should be about to come on himself right about now,' Virgil thought as she walked over to him. "Sorry to interrupt, but I'm going to go to the bathroom." She pulled down her panties before closing the door.

Larry saw this and couldn't seem to concentrate very well after that, he kept making mistakes and starting over just to make another mistake.

"Is everything okay with you?" asked Liza.

"I'm okay, it's just that sometimes I get stuck. I'll get it right in a minute."

At that moment, Virgil walked out of the bathroom and over to where Larry was drawing she bent over to get a good look at what he was doing, exposing her breast and letting them hang out.

This time, she didn't leave it at that, she stooped under his arms with her back to him and, facing Liza.

"Let me help you," she said, pushing up against his well-swelled cock. "Let's see, where you are having the problem? I will fix it for you, and you can observe." Virgil spread her legs slightly before she begin to draw.

Larry then eased his hand up her skirt and pulled her panties down half way. He played with her clit until her juices dripped into his hand. Virgil continued to draw as if it didn't affect her.

Larry dropped down in front of Virgil and inhaled her essence while he nibbled on her slippery clit. Now at this point, Virgil herself was having a hard time drawing. She spread her legs wider, letting Larry know that he was invited.

Virgil also dropped the brush and started running her fingers through Larry's hair. He then picked her up and carried her over to the bed. Liza came over and chipped in by helping Larry remove his pants.

On the other side of the bed, Virgil was yanking off her panties and tearing off her blouse. Soon she was naked as the day that she was born. Virgil and Liza looked at each other and then at Larry, to whom still had his socks and underwear on.

"This isn't fair," said Liza.

"We all should get naked," said Virgil, reaching for him. He quickly moved away.

"Oh, so you want to play a game, huh?" said Liza, chasing after Larry, to whom was now skipping across the room, yelling, "Catch me if you can."

Virgil and Liza huddled together, discussing a play. Soon they had him tackled on the floor and dragged to the bed, kicking and screaming. Virgil began trying his hands to the bed, and he was face down, while Liza ripped off his red underwear and searched under his body for the big stiff.

After Virgil finish combining him to the bed posts she pushed him up on his knees and began licking around his asshole, teasing him while he moved his ass wildly in the air, she then moved to that tender spot between his inner thighs and nuts.

Larry started making squealing noises that a sad puppy makes. Virgil kept up the tease, she took her tongue back to his asshole making slow circular movements. When she thought he couldn't take it anymore. She rammed her tongue inside, causing Larry's asshole to drip with precum.

Larry bucked wildly, making it harder for Virgil to hold on, but she didn't care. She just kept licking at his asshole until Larry cried out and was about to explode. She removed her mouth to keep the strength alive in her prey.

Larry then laid on the bed while Liza untied his hands, he thought of both pussies and realized how lucky he was. He first sucked Liza's clit, then slowly made it down to her wet, juicy house of lava.

He then admired Virgil's tight ass and moved down to her wet, juicy hole. He kept the tease up until Virgil reached back and grabbed his rod of pleasure and eagerly guided it into her waiting mouth.

Liza watched while Larry's cock slid in and out of Virgil's mouth, making her clit pound like a heartbeat. Liza positioned herself on top of Virgil's soft ass, moving her pearl tongue in a circular movement on her cheeks, sending tornado waves of pleasure throughout her body.

Liza moaned as she rolled on Virgil's ass and Larry fucked her in the mouth. Liza's moans made Larry pump harder. Upon reaching his peak of climaxing, his body shivered like an earthquake.

It's your turn, Liza get on your knees," Virgil ordered. Liza was on her knees with the quickness and Virgil began licking Liza's neglected pussy. Liza's ass moved all about while Virgil fucked her hot pussy with her tongue. Virgil then begin to tease her by withdrawing most of her tongue, making Liza stick her ass out farther.

Larry watched in amazement. He couldn't believe his eyes. "Suck my head. Don't forget about me over here," Larry blurred out.

"No way, you're not going to come again without giving me some of that dick," said Liza. Virgil ignored Larry's plea and continued to lick Liza's pussy all the way to the big one. After Liza's dam broke, and she was stretched out on the bed.

Larry was ready for some action from the main course.

"Stack yourselves," said Larry. Virgil and Liza got on their knees, one on top of the other. Larry admired both of their pussies at first before fucking them both into a double spasm of pleasure.

For a while, everyone just laid there without moving until Liza, whom was at the bottom, began complaining about being cramped. Larry rolled over, and within seconds, he was asleep. Liza and Virgil seized the opportunity to slip out without making a sound.

Liza and Virgil were having lunch the next day when the subject of the mini orgy that they had with Larry came up.

"So, Liza, what did you think about last night?"

"That was great."

"Do you think that there are a lot of people in this world who are having as much fun as we are?" asked Virgil.

"Oh, I hope so. If not, they don't know what they're missing."

"Hey, Liza, if I tell you something, will you promise that you'll never tell another soul?"

"I will never tell."

"Well, I guess I can trust you. Last weekend when Steve was here, he came up with the conclusion that we shouldn't be afraid to explore our deepest fantasies, and we did."

"What do you mean you did?" asked Liza. "I want facts and details, honey."

"Gosh, you are so nosy. Anyway, what I mean by that is . . . okay, I will put it to you like this. Steve set it up so that Keair and I were on the balcony, fucking, while he was in the closet with the camcorder."

Liza's mouth dropped opened. She didn't say anything for a few seconds.

"You did what?" screamed Liza, not believing what she'd just heard.

"I sucked and fucked Keair on my balcony while Steve filmed it."

"What in the hell are you two doing?"

"Do you find something wrong with it?" Steve and I had sex afterwards."

Liza's mouth dropped open again. "You guys have really gone mad this time, Virgil."

"You haven't heard the best part yet."

"I don't think I want to hear this one."

"I'm going to tell you anyway. Brace yourself. I called an old schoolmate of mine from out of town. He sucked Steve's dick while I was in the closet watching."

Liza's neck snapped back into amazement. She gave Virgil the strangest look. "Virgil, I hate to ask you this, but have you and Steve been doing drugs or something like that?

There is no way I would let someone else fuck my John while I watch, no sirree, said Liza. "Well, since you guys are getting your fantasies on, are you going to tell him about your most recent ones?"

"No, and neither are you. What he doesn't know won't hurt him and he must never be told."

Okay, your secret is safe with me."

I miss him so much. I may fool around with other men, but Steve is my one and only true love. None of them can ever take his place.

That's why I've been thinking a lot lately about taking a little trip and surprising him."

"To Africa?" Liza asked.

"Yes, to Africa."

"Virgil, you can't go to Africa."

"And why not?"

"Because I can't go," said Liza.

"Look, Liza, your man is here already. Mine is not. As a matter of fact, he is so far away that I can only talk to him once a week."

"Well, how long are you going to be gone?"

"I don't know, but I won't be leaving yet. First, I'm going to give Steve a chance to miss me, and then I'll just show up and shock his system unannounced."

Liza gave Virgil a big hug. "I'll miss you, sis."

Virgil squeezed Liza harder. "I'll miss you too.

Chapter 5

Virgil was not amused when she woke up in the middle of the night to find Liza's hair stuck to her face. She tried to move backwards, but bumped into something hard behind her.

Turning her head slowly to the left, there was John, sleeping silently with his mouth wide open.

With a crazy thought inside of her head, Virgil first pushed John then Liza out of her bed. They both hit the floor with a thump.

"Virgil, why did you do that?" asked John, still half asleep.

"What happened?" asked Liza as she tried to get up off the floor.

Virgil laughed. "You should have seen your faces."

"What's so funny about throwing us out of bed?" asked John.

"Make sure that you label it right. It's my bed and I threw you out because I couldn't even move my legs. You guys were making a bolognea sandwich out of me.

Out of all the rooms in this house, you just happened to find yourselves in this one."

"Let's go, John. We know when we're not welcome." Liza picked her clothes up off the floor and stuck her tongue out at Virgil.

"Wait!" Virgil screamed. John and Liza turned around.

"April and I are going on a picnic tomorrow. If you unwanted people want to join us, you can." There was no reply as John and Liza turned around quickly and disappeared down the stairs.

Virgil stared in the direction of the door for a few seconds before she flopped back onto her bed, spread her arms and her legs, and pretended to be a snow angel. 'This is much better,' she thought.

Virgil got out of her bed the next morning feeling refreshed. 'Today is such a beautiful day, I'd better get out of this bed, take advantage of the day and take April out for her routine stroll before I go to the park. After Virgil was dressed, Ana walked in with April along with an outfit for her to wear.

Ana was assisting Virgil in getting April dressed.

"Ana, have you seen April's yellow sun cap, the one that Mom and Dad, brought back from the Lake Tahoe trip?"

"Yes, Mrs. Virgil, I last saw it downstairs inside April's playpen."

"Oh, thank you." "Will you hold April while I go downstairs and get it?" Virgil gave the baby to Ana, she ran down the steps two at a time, and grabbed the cap out of the playpen.

She noticed her dad talking to a strange man just outside by the pool. 'Must be new hired help,' she thought, as she skipped back up stairs, putting April in her stroller and taking the elevator down.

Virgil strolled April out towards the pool to be nosy about the new help. The man and her father were having a drink by the beautiful aqua water.

"Hi Dad," said Virgil, walking over and giving her dad a kiss.

"Hi, baby." Her dad kissed her back. "There's someone here that I want you to meet. This is Pedro, the new pool man. Pedro, this is my daughter Virgil and my granddaughter, April."

"Hello," said Pedro. "It's nice to finally meet you."

"It's nice to meet you too."

"He'll be staying in the pool house in case you see an unfamiliar face walking around the grounds," said Dad.

"What a beautiful little girl. I love children. May I hold her for a minute?" Pedro asked.

"Go ahead, if she lets you. April sort of has her own picks and choosing to whom she likes and dislikes."

"I have a good way with kids, although I don't have any myself, so she probably won't mind." Pedro bent over and carefully lifted April out of the stroller. "Ah, she is so pretty."

And look at those fat legs and cheeks!" Pedro looked at April in amazement. "She favors you, you know."

"Why, thank you," said Virgil, blushing from ear to ear. "Well, I'd better go and let you two get back to business," Virgil took April from Pedro.

"Goodbye," said Pedro.

Virgil moved April's arm to wave back at Pedro.

That night, Virgil tossed and turned in her sleep. She just couldn't get comfortable for anything. Getting out of bed, she decided to go down stairs to get a glass of warm milk.

Passing the patio window, she noticed the curtains were partially opened and the full moon was beaming in. Just as she began to open the curtains wider to get a better look at the moon, she saw the new help, Pedro, skinny-dipping in the pool.

Virgil's eyes widened. "Get out of the pool," she kept whispering to herself so that she could see what he was packing, but Pedro just kept on swimming.

An half an hour had passed and Virgil got really tired of waiting, so finally she gave up and went on to the kitchen for her milk.

Coming back from the kitchen, she looked through the patio door again and Pedro was nowhere to be seen. "Shit!" she said aloud. 'I knew that was going to happen. If I'd just stayed a little while longer,' she thought.

After a few more minutes of waiting, Virgil removed herself from the window and went back upstairs to her bedroom.

Once again in her bed, Virgil was still unable to sleep. She tried counting sheep balloons, reading, and watching a little T.V., but nothing worked.

Looking out of her bedroom window, she saw a light on in the pool house. Creeping downstairs and out the door, Virgil decided that she was going to peep inside to see what Pedro was doing up at this time of night.

Peeking through the sliding doors, she could see Pedro with a white towel around his waist, and cooking something on the stove. Then something strange happened; he disappeared into the back.

Upon returning, he turned off the stove without even checking the food and went into the back again, this time for at least twenty minutes.

For Virgil, twenty minutes was a long time to be standing outside in front of someone's private domain in night clothes.

She finally gave up once again and started walking towards the house. When she arrived in front of the picnic table, Pedro grabbed her from behind and put his hand over her mouth.

"I saw you watching me. Did you like what you saw?" Virgil jerked his hand from over her mouth.

"I couldn't see anything." Virgil could feel the bulge through Pedro's clothing and through her nightshirt as well.

Pedro spread Virgil's legs with his foot, then slowly licked around her outer earlobe with the tip of his tongue. "Are you thinking about this tongue going in and out, around and around, and up and down your hot snatch?"

With his free hand, he gently rubbed Virgil's pearl tongue through her soft silk panties. Virgil moaned helplessly. He licked his fingers before putting them down inside her panties, touching her thrill of excitement.

He released her, unbuttoned her night shirt, pulled it off her arms and placed it on the table beside them. Virgil didn't speak. Pedro then withdrew his hot pistol and rolled it all over Virgil's back, ass, and down between her legs.

"Bend over," he demanded. She obeyed. He rolled his bare dick over Virgil's ass again, making her pussy really wet. She reached back to grab him, but he pushed her hand away.

"Don't move," he said, Bending his knees slightly while rubbing his cock along the outside of her aching slit, allowing her juices to drip all over him.

Virgil began to move her ass around. She wanted it, but every time she tried to grab him, he just pushed her hand away.

Pedro rose up, removed his clothes and turned Virgil around to face him. Virgil blinked her eyes twice before she finally got her first official look at Pedro's naked body.

It was hard all over, and that dick. It stood straight out, big and long with a curve to get to every notch and cranny.

Virgil's heart was beating very fast, chills shot up and down her spine.

"Put one leg on the bench and let me get a better feel of your wet pussy."

Virgil obeyed. Pedro rammed three fingers inside of Virgil's hot box. "Someone give me a cup," he said sarcastically.

"I hope that my dick is big enough for you." Pedro let it wave from side to side, showing off his dick control. I bet you don't know anyone that can do that. "You want to touch it, don't you? Go ahead, you can touch me."

Virgil hesitated.

"Go ahead, he don't bite."

Virgil grabbed it with both hands, feeling every vein and the smoothness of his skin. She got on her knees to suck it.

"That's enough, I think that you'd better go now." Pedro helped Virgil up and back into her nightshirt. But before he pulled up her panties, he stuck his finger up her cunt one more time and rubbed the juices on the head of his dick, then walked away.

Virgil was completely confused. 'What in the hell was that?' she asked to herself as she walked back to her room. She kept looking over her shoulders, hoping that he'd change his mind and come after her, but he didn't.

Virgil removed her clothes once again and threw them hard against the chair next to her bed. Stepping into the shower, she removed the showerhead from its place and adjusted it to a medium flow, massaging every aspect of her body.

When Virgil thought she was at the peak of climaxing, she turned the water down just a little lower. She parted her pussy cheeks to expose her pointed clit to the spray of the water, closed her eyes, and tilted her head back. 'That hits the spot,' she thought.

With visions in her head of Pedro's hard dick and body, she imagined that he was fucking her. He leaned her over the picnic table with the soft breeze of the wind skiing across her bare ass, and then plunging his hard shaft into her waiting cunt, sending tiny sharp tingles all over her body.

As Virgil's mind went on with the fantasy, her breast nipples grew hard. She grabbed one, put it into her mouth, and nibbled on it, sending streams of lightning all the way down to her fingertips.

Her pussy was about to explode with all of this excitement going on. She opened her pussy cheeks wider, truly not missing the target now.

She moved her body around and around while making love to the showerhead until she exploded into a downstream, making her body quiver.

After all of that she took a quick shower and got into bed. She was now tired, and sure that she could go to sleep without counting sheep.

The next morning Virgil and Liza went for a swim and Pedro walked over and stood by the diving board.

"How are you two doing today?" asked Pedro.

"Fine," answered Liza. "Won't you come in and have a swim with us?"

"Maybe later on my lunch break. There's something that I need to do right now. Besides, I don't think your father would like me slipping up on the job."

"When's your break?" asked Liza.

"In about an hour."

"Liza," Virgil broke in. "I don't think Mr. Pedro would like to spend his lunch hour swimming in a pool. He probably has other things to do, like harass the innocent maids."

"I have an hour and a half lunch break. I had planned to sit in this pool and read the paper anyway, swim a little, and then eat lunch. That's if it's okay with you guys."

"Oh, it's okay," said Liza.

"What about you, Virgil, is it okay for me to sit in the same pool with you and read the paper?" asked Pedro as he stood over Virgil's head.

"You're the pool man. I'm quite sure you can sit in this pool if you want."

Pedro leaned down closer to Virgil's ear. "That's wasn't the question. The question was, do you or do you not want me to take a break here?"

Virgil turned to look up at him. "Do whatever you want."

"I know why you're a little salty with me. That explains your attitude. I don't blame you for being angry, but if you keep it up, you'll never get this dick, and I know you want it, so don't give me that look."

"Do what you want," said Virgil.

"Okay, then it is settled. I'll see you two guys in less than an hour."

After Pedro left. Liza looked at Virgil in confusion. "What was that all about?"

"Nothing."

"You're lying, Virgil."

"What makes you say that?"

"Because I know you. Have you guys met in between the time that Dad introduced you and now?"

"No, Liza."

"I don't believe you, I tell you what, I will talk, and you can say whether I'm right or wrong." "Did you fuck him?"

"Wrong."

"Did you sucked his dick?"

"Wrong."

"Okay, Okay, I've got it. You saw him fucking one of the maids, and you wanted him first."

"Liza, what have I told you about your brain? It wasn't like that. I did see him last night, but I didn't get a chance to fuck him."

"And why not, girl?"

"Because he didn't let me. He's a manipulator, a teaser, and anything else that goes with that category. He's trying to play with my mind."

Liza looked confused and was still uncertain about what had actually taken place. "So what did happen?"

"I was walking in front of the picnic table about three a.m. this morning."

"Wait, wait, wait, back up. Why were you outside alone at that time of the morning?"

"Never mind that part. But anyway, to make a long story short, he pulled down my panties, rolled his dick all over my ass and between my legs, showed the dick to me, and helped me get dressed."

"Wait, Virgil! Are you holding out again? You mean to tell me that he did all of that and didn't give it to you?"

Virgil nodded. "Yes!" "That's exactly what happened."

"I'd be a little pissed too. I know what, we can get the extra key to the pool house. We'll go over there in the middle of the night, tie him up, and jump his bones."

"Liza, give your brain a rest, because it's putting in too much unnecessary time again."

"Virgil, I have one more question though?"

"What is it?"

"How big was this dick of his?"

"It was huge, I wanted it so bad. The head on it was large. I could feel every vein. He let me touch it and that made me want it even more."

"But, he wouldn't let you have it?"

"No, he wouldn't, I told you that he's just a teaser."

"So what are we going to do?"

"You can try to see how far you can get with him; but me, I'm staying away, far away. Seems to me that he has played this sort of game before."

"The next time that he goes into that shed, I'll make my move on him. Watch and learn sis."

"Here's your chance, Liza, because he just went in the shed."

Liza got out of the pool and made her way inside the tool shed.

"Hi again," said Liza, as she entered the shed.

"What are you doing here, Liza?"

"Oh, I just came to see what you were doing. As she moved in a few feet away from him.

My bathing suit is very easy to come off, all you have to do is pull a few strings," said Liza, getting right to the point.

"Liza, I don't think that this is the right time."

"Time? Oh we have plenty of time," she said moving closer and beginning to unzip Pedro's overall's and released his nature's pole. "Wow! You are big!

How about a quickie before lunch?" asked Liza, to whom at this point began peeling off her bathing suit, removing Pedro's overalls, and pushing him in the chair just behind him. She attempted to straddle Pedro.

But, Pedro acted quickly by flipping Liza over his knee, laying her on his lap, and making sure that her clit was directly on his cock.

He then began to spank her, and every time that his hand made contact with her ass, it gave her body a tingle that put goose bumps, to shame. Liza tried to get away, but he had a tight hold on her and she couldn't go anywhere.

After he finished spanking her, Pedro took the privilege of sticking his middle finger up her cunt. "You're all wet, Liza, Does that mean that you liked it?"

Liza was furious. She threw on her bathing suit, stomped out of the shed, and got back into the pool beside Virgil.

Virgil smiled at Liza. "What happened? From the look on your face it seems to me that he showed you how it was done."

"You were right, he is an asshole, I took off my bathing suit, and he spanked me."

Virgil laughed. "Your plan didn't work, huh?"

"Virgil, what are we going to do about this Pedro person?"

"Nothing. As a matter of fact, I think that we should just play along with him like nothing happened."

"Are you kidding? I've got to get him back for doing that to me."

"Just be cool, I'm sure between the both of us we'll be able to come up with some kind of plan."

"Here comes Mr. Mystery now," said Liza. Pedro walked over and stood at his favorite spot by the edge of the pool.

"So, are you still going to spend your break with us?" asked Virgil.

"No, I'm sorry, but you guys are going to have to take a rain check. Something came up and I won't be able to spend time with you two today."

"Oh, what a pity, I guess we'll just have to make do without you," said Liza, sarcastically.

Pedro gave Liza a mean look. "Well, I'll leave you two alone and he walked off.

"See you around," said Liza.

"Something came up," repeated Virgil. They both laughed as they watch Pedro disappear into the pool house.

A couple of days later Dad decided to invite a surprise guest to dinner. "Dad, when is this guest of yours going to show up?" asked Virgil. "I'm ready to eat dinner at anytime now." At that moment, Pedro walked quickly into the dining room.

"Shit," said Liza. "I don't believe this."

"Sorry I'm late," said Pedro.

"Oh, that's okay. You're always welcome, late or not," said Dad.

"You can sit in the empty spot on the other side of Virgil."

Virgil frowned. 'Why does he have to sit by me' she thought.

All through dinner, Pedro kept giving Virgil these funny looks and putting his hand on her lap.

Virgil turned to face Pedro. "Do you mind?" she asked, trying to hide her voice with her napkin. Pedro just smiled.

After dinner, Virgil's family was sometimes engaged in quiet time. That's when everyone went out into the courtyard. They would talk in low tones, whispers, and some didn't talk at all.

Everyone in the house at the time was invited to quiet time, including all of the hired help. That was a good thing for them. They got an extra break with pay.

Pedro looked all over the courtyard for Virgil, but he didn't see her. He was about to give up when he saw part of her skirt from behind a big tree. He walked over to her.

"So what are you doing back here all by yourself?" he asked, because he couldn't think of anything else to say.

"Just thinking."

"About what?"

"My husband."

"Oh yeah, him. I almost forgotten about him. Your dad told me all about it."

"All about what?" asked Virgil.

"You know, about your husband being on tour most of the year, but that's not too bad. At least he's making a living for you and April."

"I don't understand you, Pedro."

"What?" he asked.

"Sometimes you can say the nicest things then the next minute you're this arrogant person whom thinks that no one can touch him."

Pedro disregarded her comment.

"Your folks have a beautiful home. Maybe you can give me a tour sometime."

"Don't try to change the subject. Why are you that way with me?"

"I'm that way because I've been taken advantage of several times in my life and if I can help it, it will never happen again. I'm really a nice person on the inside, but I haven't met anyone to be nice to. But I do like you."

"You have a very unique way of showing it. I think you have, a lot of anger inside of you. I just hope it doesn't back fire. Now let's go on that tour. Quiet time is now over," explained Virgil.

Virgil played the tour guide role and escorted, Pedro throughout the whole house. She saved her room for last. "This is my room where I used to sleep when I was a little girl, and I still sleep here when Steve is away," she explained.

Virgil suddenly thought of the time. "Oh my gosh, what time is it?"

Pedro looked at his watch. "It's eight-thirty."

"You'll have to excuse me for a moment. I have to go and kiss April good night. I always try to kiss her before she's put down to bed at night. I'll be right back."

"Oh, there is a photo album in the first drawer by the bed to entertain you while I'm gone," said Virgil, before she raced out of the door.

Pedro opened the drawer. He pulled out the photo album. Underneath was a diary. Upon opening it up, the first page read, "My Fantasies."

Flipping through the pages, Pedro noticed that it was a diary that Virgil kept about her and the things that she would like to be done to her.

He stuck the book in the back of his pants and pretended to be looking in the middle of the photo album when she returned.

"I have a big day tomorrow, so I think I'll just go home now, maybe relax a little and turn in early." Pedro stood up carefully, making sure that the book didn't show under his shirt.

"Okay." Virgil walked him to the back patio door.

As soon as Pedro shut the door to the pool house, he pulled the book from under his shirt and began to read.

Virgil, on the other hand, was so bored that she drove to John's house to see if that was where Liza went.

She banged on the door very hard. "Open this door."

"What's all the fuss about?" asked John as he opened the door. "I knew it was you. She's in the backroom."

Virgil rushed in and found Liza lounging in the den. "Liza, who gave you permission to leave, without telling me about it first?"

"Excuse me, I didn't know that I had to report to you my every move, and besides, the last time that I saw you, you were headed upstairs with that, that whatever his name is."

Virgil laughed. "I'm just kidding with you. I came over because I'm bored and I just wanted to get on your nerves, since I've no other nerves to get on."

"Ah, what's the matter? You miss your hubby?" Liza poked out her bottom lip to tease Virgil about being lonely.

"Just a little, mostly at times when I don't have anything to do," Virgil grinned. "Also, you don't have to poke your lip out so far, I'm not that sad," she said with a grin.

"So what did that man have to say while you were giving him a tour of our family house?"

"Oh, nothing much. Just something about how he's been hurt real bad in the past, but if I get to know him, he's not a bad person."

Liza was not impressed. "Oh yeah, I can't imagine that."

"Well, sometimes he says some pretty neat things."

"And the other times?" asked Liza.

"Come on, give him a chance."

"You have a crush on him, don't you, Virgil?"

"I don't know, but I do know one thing."

"What's that?"

"I can tell that he knows what he's doing when it comes down to sex," explained Virgil. "We'll have to be very careful about how we pay him back."

"Well, I'm going to go. I think John want something. He keeps looking in on us." "You know how they are when they want some," said Liza. They both laughed.

Virgil drove back to the house. She took a quick shower, then put on only panties with a small shirt to match. She had just finished dressing when she heard something outside of her balcony. Virgil took a peek outside. It was Pedro.

"Meet me at the pool house in ten minutes," said Pedro.

Arriving at the pool house in her robe and slippers. Virgil noticed that there weren't any lights turned on inside, but she went in anyway.

"Pedro? Pedro, are you here?" Virgil whispered. She tried to turn on the nearest light switch, but for some reason, it wasn't working.

Suddenly the door slammed behind her. "Oh shit," she said.

Someone attacked her from behind, putting their manly hand over her mouth, jerking off her robe and dragged her until they reached the bedroom.

He threw her on the bed face down, ripping off her panties and top. Virgil tried to flip him off of her, but he was too heavy.

She then scooted and wiggled her way to the end of the bed, with her head almost touching the floor. Suddenly, he rammed it in, only getting in two strokes before she flipped him off and he landed on the floor.

She tried for the door, but he was right behind her, slamming the door seconds after she opened it wide enough to escape. He had her pinned to the door bending his knees to try to get it in again.

Virgil wouldn't let him. She threw her body sideways and somehow they both fell. Virgil tried to crawl away.

Holding onto Virgil's ankles, Pedro pulled her back quickly, as he smothered her body; he tried again to stroke her, but Virgil kicked him off and began to run.

Pedro ran down his prey in the living room, throwing her onto the couch, pulling her back by the hips and giving it to her hard, just like he had read it in her diary, long and rough.

"Ah!" Virgil screamed, as her tits bounced wildly while he rammed his swollen cock in and out of her.

"Have you had enough of this dick?" asked Pedro between breathes.

"No," replied Virgil, "give me some more."

Pedro leaned over, almost laying on her back and began to fuck her so hard that her head was hitting the back rest of the couch. Virgil screamed in excitement as Pedro worked very hard to give her exactly what she wanted.

When the time came, Pedro squeezed Virgil's hand tightly as he ejected into a shuttle release.

Pedro and Virgil didn't move for a very long time, they thought that they'd stay there awhile and catch their breath.

Pedro was finally relaxed and he was the first to interrupt the silence that grew between them.

"Did you know that the last time I was with you, I was so hard that I had to go home and jack myself off."

"That was your decision. You wanted it that way, even though my pussy was right there for you."

"I had to check you out first. I don't like to fuck a dry pussy. But that night I was shocked to find out that you get water wet. It was hard controlling myself from taking you right then and there, especially when your cum juices dripped on my dick and in my hand.

Now, that's wasn't what I expected—at all. I almost couldn't control myself. You see, I like to be in control. I wanted you to get just a little taste of what I have so you'd come looking for me and want what I have to offer.

It was necessary to tease you then and wait for you later not to mention pounce on you like a big cat."

Minutes passed before Virgil decided that she had to leave. "I better go now, I have to meet Liza tomorrow."

"Okay," said Pedro. "I guess I'll see you later."

Virgil gathered her torn clothes and slithered like a snake into the house unnoticed.

Chapter 6

"You're late! Do you know how long it's been since I first arrived here? I've been waiting here for two hours. Where have you been?"

"I overslept," said Virgil.

"And how did you do that?" asked Liza. "Didn't you go to bed after you left my house last night?"

"Yes, I did go to bed all right."

"And what do you mean by all right, Virgil? Did you fuck Pedro last night?"

"Can we discuss this later?" asked Virgil. "I want to quickly do my shopping and get the hell out of this mall before it gets too crowded in here. You know how I hate standing in long lines."

"Okay, I've got an idea," said Liza.

"Oh my gosh!" Your brain is getting ready to put in some overtime again."

Liza gave Virgil a big push. "I was only going to say we can shop and talk at the same time because I want to know the reason behind you being late today."

"We could, but only one of us knows how to do both," said Virgil as she followed behind Liza into the nearest women's clothing store and begin to shop.

"Very funny," said Liza, letting her hands drop to her sides with the clothes still in them. "Do I have a target on my forehead or something? Now just tell me what happened, okay? Can you do that?"

"I guess you deserve to know."

Virgil smiled, "To make a long story short, Pedro came to my window. I went to the pool house, the lights were off. I couldn't get them on. Someone attacked me from behind, ripping off my clothes and fucked me doggie style."

"You get off on that, don't you, Virgil?"

"And you don't?"

"Well, that just sort of sounds like rape to me."

"Don't you see, Liza? What I did last night is in my diary. Remember?"

"You're right, I'm just thinking about you doing it for fun when some women get it for torture."

"Don't get all sentimental on me now, Liza. That was the best fuck that I've had in a long time."

You always say that. But I have one question. Did you tell him what you wanted?"

"No, and that's what made it so exciting. He gave me exactly what I always wanted but, was just too chicken to ask for it."

"I still don't trust him," said Liza.

"Don't tell me that you're still bitter over that shed thing."

"No, it isn't that. Just be careful, that's all. He's slick and I wouldn't trust him with my mind. My pool maybe, but not the mind."

"I'll be careful. Now let's hurry up and get out of here before we're late for the lingerie party. You know how Pamela is—she likes to make an all-nite event out of everything."

Liza raised one eyebrow. "Therefore we're going to need some rest. As soon as we leave here we're going to Mom and Dad's house to take a nap."

Virgil nodded her head in agreement. "I know that's right. I'm with you on that one."

An hour snooze in the afternoon was all the energy that Virgil and Liza needed before they went to the lingerie party.

Their dad was half asleep in his favorite recliner when Virgil tried to sneak by him first, with her black silk bra-like top, satin short shorts with high splits on each side, a see-through net robe with a silk belt to match, black satin slippers, and rollers in her hair.

He woke up just in time to see her trying to slip by him, "Virgil, honey." Virgil stopped in her tracks. "Where in the world are you going looking like that?"

"To a lingerie party, Daddy."

"Liza and I are late, so I decided not to take my rollers out yet. I'm going to put an oversize coat over this outfit until I get there."

"That's a relief. I guess I don't have to make that phone call, to Africa."

"Thanks, Daddy," said Virgil, and she gave him a kiss on the cheek.

"Liza, you can come out now!" Dad yelled.

Liza crept out with her tight-fitting, all-in-one red lace sheer nightie, matching red high-heeled pumps, and her hair fixed neatly in a corn roll. Dad took one look at her. "Liza, are you going to the same party as Virgil?"

"Yes daddy, I am."

Dad studied Liza from head to toe. "Are there going to be any men there?"

"No, why do you ask?"

"Uh, Virgil, you make sure that Liza has an overcoat on. We wouldn't want her insides to catch a cold." After they left, Dad mumbled to himself. "That damn girl always has to be different."

"See, I told you we should've used another door," said Liza as she and Virgil walked away quickly.

"No matter what door we used, someone was going to see us anyway. It was better for Dad to see us instead of one of the new maids, so they won't go back and tell Steve the story all wrong."

Liza and Virgil arrived at Pamela's house on time for the party.

Pamela answered the door after just one knock. "Gee, Liza, you look so good that I might want to fuck you myself."

Liza grabbed Pamela's arm and pulled her close. "Well, just in case. You never know what's going to happen." Pamela pushed her away.

"You're something else. I hope your daddy didn't see you walking out of the house with that on because, I would've liked to have seen the look on his face."

Virgil giggled. "Too late, he already saw her and you're right, you should've been there to see the look on his face."

Pamela took another look at Liza's outfit. "Liza, you know this is a lingerie party for women. As you can see, there aren't any men here."

"That's okay, I'll have room to squeeze one of you in later, so don't forget your swim suit because I might just come all over you." Everyone laughed at Liza's statement.

Pamela laughed loudly at Liza's joke. "Virgil, I just don't know what we're going to do with her."

"I don't know either but ask my dad. I know he wanted to kill her when he saw her walking out of the house dressed the way she is now."

Pamela couldn't help herself she took one more look at Liza and laughed to herself. "She's going to send your old man to an early grave." Virgil also laughed.

"What's so funny?" "You people are haters." Liza said, as she pointed towards Pamela and Virgil.

Pamela shook her head. "You two go down stairs to the basement and enjoy the party with the rest of the crew. We have a lot of things planned. Ten minutes later Pamela arrived downstairs with the last guest and made her announcement.

"Excuse me!" "Excuse me everyone!" Everybody looked in Pamela's direction. "We are going to make a night of this, no one is allowed to leave until daybreak."

"If you open the door the alarm will go off, I will not answer the phone when the alarm company calls, the cops will come, and I will tell them that I never seen you before in my life." "Now let's Party!!" she screamed.

The party lasted until daybreak, just as Pamela promised.

The sun had barely peeped through the clouds when Liza had to call John to pick them up. When he arrived and they got into the car, Liza began to scold him.

"You know you're getting just like Virgil, never on time for anything."

"Don't blame me, I didn't stay up all night getting drunk in my nightie. If you would've stayed off the booze a little, I wouldn't have to pick you up. Don't you guys know the rules? Only one can get drunk, the other one drives, it's as simple as that."

"Will you guys hold down your lovers' quarrel? I'm trying to get some sleep here," said Virgil as she laid stretched out in the backseat.

As soon as John begin to drive, Liza slowly took off her shoes, removed her outfit, and flung her underwear onto the dashboard.

Locking the door behind her, she leaned back in her seat and gapped her legs open as wide as she could, without putting one foot on the floor.

John looked over at her.

"Keep your eyes on the road, John." John watched Liza stick two fingers inside of her cunt and then suck them both. His dick grew hard.

John took a deep swallow as he tried to keep one eye on the road, and the other one on Liza's pussy.

Liza scooted over so that her pussy was closer to John. He reached out to touch it.

Liza slapped his hand. "Nope, look but don't touch."

He jerked his hand back in pain. "That's not fair!"

"Life isn't fair," Liza, stretched one leg out and began rubbing his cock with her toes. She felt his dick grow harder. She then raised the other foot up near his face.

John stretched out his neck to grab Liza's big toe with his mouth, and when he was close to nabbing it, she jerked it back just in time.

"Stop teasing before we have a wreck." She put her foot up there again, this time she let John catch it with his soft lips and he begin to suck her toes and every slot in between. Liza continued to massage his dick with her other foot.

After a while, John let Liza's toes go, and she moved close enough to let him finger-fuck her. Liza met every thrust of his three fingers and was on her way to an orgasm when John pulled up in front of Virgil's house.

"We're here, sleepyhead," said Liza, leaning back and screaming into Virgil's right ear.

"We're here already?" said Virgil as she wiped her eyes and slowly got out of the car. "See you later," she managed to squeeze out just before a big yawn.

Virgil slowly stumbled into the house.

"Gosh, somebody needs to go to the grocery store," said Virgil, as she looked in the refrigerator for a snack and couldn't find anything. "I guess that's what you get when you're never home," she said to herself.

Virgil carefully walked upstairs, taking off her clothes along the way. She fell onto the bed on her stomach, naked. One more hour and then I'll go and get April, she thought, as she laid there, too lazy to move.

Only ten minutes into her sleep, Virgil began to dream. Her ass rose up and down in the air, she spread her legs and ass cheeks, moving around and around in a circular motion, before rolling over, raising her knees up, and massaging her clit with one hand and probing her breast with the other.

She then held one breast in her mouth with one hand while the other hand was free to continue to probe between her legs, rubbing up and down on her swollen snatch.

Rolling back onto her stomach, she then bunched up the covers into a tight ball and begin to hump it wildly, putting both hands under the bulge to make it harder.

She was on her way to her sexual peak when there was a knock at the door. Virgil grabbed a robe.

She opened the door and a familiar face appeared. "Pedro?" Virgil whispered. "Who let you in?"

"Charles did," replied Pedro.

'Charles is fired,' Virgil thought to herself. "Why are you here?" she asked.

"Your mom wanted you to know that she and your father are taking April to a reunion with them tonight. They want to show her off."

"Okay, thanks for telling me. Now, if it's okay with you, I'd like to go back to sleep," said Virgil, kind of upset because he'd disturbed her dream.

"Are you sure that you want me to go?" asked Pedro. He glanced at the bed and noticed the bulge; and also at the fact that part of her breast was showing.

"I'm sure," said Virgil.

Pedro moved very close to her. "You know, Virgil, this dick will feel far better than any old covers." He placed Virgil's hand on the knot in his pants. "Feel how big and hard this is. It's waiting for you, but it wants you to baby it first though."

"Baby it? What do you mean by that?"

"It wants you to suck it," said Pedro, whipping it out.

"I'm not sucking it."

"You will," ordered Pedro. He pushed her up against the wall, untying her robe and nibbling gently on her breast, while letting his rod massage her hot pearl tongue.

"Are you ready to baby my dick yet?" asked Pedro.

"No," replied Virgil. "Baby your own dick."

Pedro dropped down to his knees, grabbed her legs and began to eat her pussy. Virgil squirmed and wiggled, but he wouldn't let her go.

Pedro asked Virgil again. "Are you ready to suck me off?"

"No," replied Virgil softly. "I'm not giving in."

Pedro picked her up and dropped her on the bed softly. "You're a very bad girl." He tied her hands to the bedpost and only stuck the tip of his dick head inside of her hotbox.

Virgil raised her body up to meet his, but he only pulled away.

Virgil relaxed and starred into Pedro's eyes. He stuck the tip of his dick inside of her again and started to fuck her that way.

"Give it to me," said Virgil. Pedro ignored her and begin to nibble on her nipples while he fucked her with only the tip of the head inside. Virgil couldn't stand it any longer.

Virgil cried out. "Fine, I'll suck it."

"Too late," Pedro took his head out and begin to rub it against the entrance of her milk hole. Virgil moved her head from side to side and arched her back to meet his love toy.

"Please, I'll suck it good for you."

"Real good?" asked Pedro.

Virgil shook her head in agreement. Pedro eased his dick into her mouth, moving slowly at first until Virgil begin to hit that spot on his dick head that he had no control over. Pedro gave out a little moan and began to pump faster into Virgil's mouth.

Virgil got this yearning between her legs as she watched Pedro's ass hump up and down in the ceiling mirror, as he fucked her mouth like he would her pussy.

Pedro started to get to excited, he was getting off into it, making those faces as if he were coming. Virgil didn't want him to come yet, so she begin to make little signals with her eyes and bounced her feet on the bed.

But he didn't pay her any attention. She couldn't even use her hands because they were tied tightly to the damn bed. 'What can I do?' she asked herself. Her pussy ached for his dick to be inside of her.

Virgil wanted him to fuck her so bad, that the only way that she was going to get his attention was to scrape her teeth on his dick. Not enough to injury him, but enough to get her point across.

Ouch! "My dick is not to be eaten with your teeth," said Pedro, as he untied her and dragged her down to the end of the bed by the ankles and raised her legs up over his shoulder's, giving Virgil just what she wanted.

Virgil's twat grew very hot while she watched his big dick drill in and out of her. Pedro made these strange faces when he was getting some monkey, sexy faces.

Virgil loved it and she begin to meet him, thrust for thrust. Suddenly Pedro's ass cheeks tightened and he started to fuck her faster than before.

Virgil could feel him inside of her stomach, while watching his ass go up and down faster and faster as he fucked her hard and long.

"Do you want me to come?" asked Pedro. Virgil dropped her legs and wrapped them around Pedro's body. I take that as a yes so hold on tight because here it c-c-co-omes."

Pedro came with such a blast that Virgil felt his liquid as it entered her insides.

Two weeks later, Virgil sat on the side of bathtub for a long time, thinking about Steve and what had been going on with her and Pedro. For some reason, she found herself thinking deeply about Pedro, and wanting him in her bed at night.

Sometimes when she was alone, she wished Pedro was around to sneak up behind her and fuck her brains out.

Just then Liza interrupted Virgil's thoughts. "Knock, knock." Liza didn't wait for a response from Virgil, she just walked in and jumped up on the counter top.

"Come in, since you're already inside. What if I was masturbating or something?" asked Virgil.

"Well, I'd just get the camcorder and watch." They both laughed.

"I've never known you to stay in this big old house by yourself this long while Steve is gone." said Liza. "What's going on?"

"I'm thinking about taking that trip to see Steve sooner than planned."

Liza folded her arms. "What made you think about this? It's Pedro, isn't it?"

"Yes, it is. I have to get away from him, I think I've been dickwhipped by the pool man. You just don't know him, Liza, he has sexual powers and dick control out of this world.

He doesn't come unless I want him to and every time that he moves, my whole body tingles. He seems to know my every desire, my every fantasy, and he knows how I want it and when I want it.

How can I take back control, when he is giving it to me like that?" asked Virgil.

"Hold up, Virgil. How does he happen to know what you want? Have you guys been talking or planning to fuck before hand? I mean, maybe he's God-given to women, but I smell something fishy. Has he ever been in your room?"

"Yes, he has, but only to look at photos in my photo album, and I only left him alone for a short time . . . Oh shit, I told him to take the photo album out of the drawer. Underneath it was my diary of all my fantasies, damn!"

"Come on, Virgil, I told you that I didn't trust him. We have to get him back for this one."

"Okay, I'm with you," said Virgil, putting suds all over Liza's hand as they shook. "It's a deal."

Liza smiled and grabbed a towel to dry her hands. "Let's go and do this." Virgil followed Liza outside into the barn. They worked on their surprise plan to greet him when he arrived.

It didn't take long for two genius minds to come up with the ultimate plan. "Is everything ready?" asked Virgil.

"Yes, it is girl."

"Here he comes," said Virgil.

Liza was thrilled. "Let's let him have it good."

Pedro entered the barn to get some work done. "Pedro, I have something to talk to you about," said Virgil.

"What's up?" asked Pedro.

"Well, I'm leaving in a couple of days, and I don't know whether or not I'm going to see you before I leave or maybe never again. Therefore, I like the way that you fuck me, and I'd like it very much if you would fuck me right now."

"Here, in the barn? "But I'm not on lunch break, and I don't won't to get into any trouble with your father."

"Don't worry about my father. He's gone for the day, so you can take as long as a break that you want," Virgil, moved a little closer to Pedro. "I want to tryout a fantasy of mine on you, but you'll have to pull off your shirt first.

I'll have to tie you up," said Virgil.

Pedro allowed Virgil to tie his hands together.

"Now, that's better," Virgil said as she finished her square knot. She made Pedro put his hands high up above his head and hooked the knot on a parallel pole just over his head. That was Liza's cue to enter the room.

"Pedro," shouted Liza from behind one of the horse's stalls' she was wearing the same bikini that she had on that day in the shed when he spanked her.

Pedro looked at Virgil. "What is she doing here?" Virgil turned to faced Pedro.

"She's my sister and besides, she wants to be here. And, you want her to be here too."

Pedro didn't respond.

"Don't tell me that you don't have fantasies of fucking us both at the same time," said Virgil.

"Wait! Don't answer that," replied Liza, waving a book in the air. "Do you recognize this book, Pedro?"

"Yes. How did you get it?"

"The same way that you took Virgil's diary, I just picked it up. So now how does it feel when the shoe is on the other foot?"

"Now we know how you think and what you want," said Virgil.

Liza was enjoying every minute of Pedro grief. "Are those ropes tight enough for you? Because according to your journal, you like them loose, but we're going to keep them a little snugged to be on the safe side." Liza gave Pedro a little whack on the buttocks with a newly purchased stuccopaddle.

"I hope this is the right kind of paddle, I'd hate to ruin your thrill," said Liza, giving him another whack. Virgil, on the other hand, begin to undo his trousers and slipped them off and over his feet, leaving him hanging there in just his underwear.

Virgil took one look at Pedro's boxers and said. "Is something wrong with your undies or are you very glad to see me."

Pedro was beginning to hate this game. "Virgil, untie me."

"No, you see, I can't do that. We haven't even started to have fun yet." Virgil opened a bottle of lotion and pulled Pedro's love tool from inside of the opening in the front of his underwear, and massaged it softly and slowly.

"How does it feel?" Pedro didn't reply. "If you don't answer, I'll have Liza come over here and spank you."

Liza didn't wait for permission as she began to spank Pedro hard.

"Ouch!" cried Pedro. You did that on purpose.

"I'm sorry," Liza giggled. "Did I hit you too hard?"

"Just go easy with that thing, will you?"

"Sure," said Liza, giving him an even harder whack.

Liza and Virgil faced each other and laughed. "Let the games begin," said Virgil.

Virgil let go of Pedro's penis placing it back where she found it and sat on the stool in front of him, but out of arm's reach. She spread her legs a little and slowly pulled her skirt up a couple of inches, rubbing her hands up and down the inside of her thighs and cupping her breast.

She then removed her loose-fitting blouse to reveal her nice rounded nipples.

Raising one up to her mouth, she sucked and licked on it, growing warmer every second, gapping her legs a little wider, and moving her hands back down to her skirt, she eased it up high, showing all that she could.

Liza jerked down Pedro's underwear, letting his hard dick go free. It stood straight out in attention, and was ready for action.

Virgil scooted down in her chair, and grabbing the back of the seat with both hands, she began throwing her pussy at him.

"Untie me," Pedro demanded.

"No way." Liza pulled off her bathing suit, and straddled a stool on the side of Virgil, and began to move back and forth, on the chair, moaning loudly.

Pedro couldn't stand watching the two of them carrying on this way, and he tried to get away, but the ropes were too tight. This drove him crazy.

As they changed positions, Liza was on her knees holding open one ass cheek with one finger and finger-fucking herself with another, while Virgil had straddled one arm of the chair and was fucking it wildly.

Pedro tried desperately to free himself again as precum juices covered the head of his dick.

"Will somebody untie these gotdamn ropes?" screamed Pedro.

Liza and Virgil both stopped and looked at each other.

"Pedro is a little cranky today," said Liza, moving her stool really close behind him. Virgil moved her stool closer in front of him.

"Just the right height, huh Liza?" said Virgil.

"You know it," said Liza as she began to fuck Pedro's nice ass cheeks, giving her a bitter sweet warm feeling between her legs than what she was getting down on the floor.

Virgil kept rubbing her juices all over his dick and every once in a while sticking the tip of her tongue in his little tight dick hole.

"Untie me. This is not funny anymore," said Pedro, now moving back and forth, because he wanted some really bad. But, Virgil just moved back to the end of the stool and grabbed his throbbing dick with one hand and fingered her swollen clit with the other until she came into a liquefying come.

After seeing the look on Pedro's face, Virgil thought it would be nice to stick two fingers up her cunt and smooth cum all over Pedro's lips.

"Virgil, please let me just stick the head in, I just want to stick my head in one time and pull it back out," begged Pedro, as he looked helpless, hanging up there with his long rod hard and his hands tied. Virgil and Liza looked at one another again.

"What do you think?" asked Virgil.

"I think it's time," said Liza. Virgil bent over in front of Pedro, pulled back her pussy lips and as soon as Pedro stuck the tip of the head in, Virgil jumped forward and Pedro came all over himself.

Liza laughed. "You're all wet," she said. "Come on, Virgil, I think our work here is finished."

"I think so too." Virgil picked up her clothes and put them back on.

Liza waved goodbye to Pedro. "We'll see you later alligator."

Pedro tried to untie himself out of his unfortunate predicament but struggling only made the ropes tighter. "You can't leave me this way."

"We already busted our nuts, we don't need yours anymore," said Liza.

"He means that we should cut him down," said Virgil.

"Oh," Liza walked over and pulled out a big butcher knife. Pedro jumped back and closed his eyes. "Don't worry, I'm only going to cut the ropes, I might want to do this again. Liza sliced the ropes with one swipe. Nice fucking with you," she said.

Virgil grinned. "See you around, Pedro."

Liza put her bathing suit back on. "I'm proud of you, sis," she said, putting her arms around Virgil's waist as they walked happily out of the barn.

Chapter 7

The time had come for Virgil to leave the States and go to the motherland.

"Virgil, honey, I wish that you wouldn't take April with you. You will only be there a little over a month or so, I wish you would leave her here with your father and me.

I won't be able to sleep at night with my grandbaby way over there in some strange, out-of-reach land. Don't you watch television? I don't want April to get sick or something," explained Mom.

"Mom, we're not going to that part, April and I'll be staying on the other side it's safer where we're going."

Mom was still very concerned. "It's still dangerous over there, no matter where you go. Your father and I will feel much better if you'd leave our only granddaughter here with us. Because if it's up to Liza, we will never get another one, so think about it, dear."

"Okay, I will," said Virgil silently. A few minutes passed. "You win again, I'll let Steve know that April isn't coming." Mom jumped up and down in excitement. Virgil did a gesture that made her eyes rolled in the back of her head. But she knew that her mother was right.

The plane ride to Africa was long and not too boring since Virgil flew first class. She didn't get much sleep, but she watched plenty of movies, and sometimes the movies ended up watching her.

Since Virgil has been convinced not to bring April, it was easy for her to have a cocktail or two. She also brought little bottles of alcohol for souvenirs. Virgil drank quite a few Virgin cocktails just for pretend.

After thirteen hours on the plane. Steve was there to greet Virgil at the airport.

"So how was your trip, babe?" Steve stood in the entrance way of the trolley bus (that brought them to the front of the airport) to help Virgil get off safely with all of her things.

"The plane ride was great, couldn't have been better. The bus ride, between airports, on the other hand, was bumpy, hot, and stinky."

Steve laughed. "What did you expect?"

"I don't know." Virgil shook her head. "I just don't know, I thought I'd take a slow bus ride part of the way so that I could take some pictures.

But I think I should have taken that private plane that you had waiting for me back in Kenya and taken pictures later."

Virgil and Steve arrived at a high-end hotel on the outskirts of Nairobi just a few hours later.

"This is a nice room," said Virgil. "I like it."

"Good, I'm glad. I was hoping that you would," Steve gave her a big hug. "I missed you, Virgil."

"I missed you too, Steve," said Virgil, flopping down in the nearest chair.

"Oh no, let's get you out of those dusty clothes first and into a nice cool bath before you start your nap."

When Virgil went into the bathroom and saw that her bathwater was already waiting for her. She removed her clothes and got in. Steve was pleased. "There, while you're soaking in here with a magazine, I'll unpack your things and put them away, and if you are good, I'll even bathe you myself"

"Sounds fair," said Virgil, sliding down into the tub so that her whole face and head could get wet. After the dip, Virgil wiped her face and hands with a dry towel and begin to read.

Twenty minutes later, Steve came into the bathroom.

"Are you ready for your bath now?" Steve, put his hands in the water and between Virgil's legs, pretending to be looking for the towel.

"Yes, I'm ready."

Steve gave Virgil a good scrub, then lifted her out of the tub, dried her off, and dressed her for bed.

"Would you like something to eat or drink?" asked Steve.

"No, thank you, I would like to just lie down, I'm a little tired. Would you like to lie down and talk with me until I fall asleep?"

"Sure, hon, I will," Steve laid down on top of the covers beside her.

"I heard that Mom talked you out of bringing April."

"I'm kind of glad she did, because if she would have came, I wouldn't have taken the bus. But the ride over here was still long, and sooner or later, she would have started getting cranky on me."

"Yes, that would've been something, especially since you couldn't bring her favorite playpen along."

"At first, it seemed like a good idea to bring her with me, but now that I'm here, it doesn't seem like a good idea anymore. Do you understand what I'm trying to say?" said Virgil.

"I wanted her to be here too, but I don't think April would have wanted a couple of doctors holding her down to give her all of those shots for the trip."

"She would have had a fit," said Virgil.

Soon Virgil began to grow very sleepy. Her eyelids began to close awhile and then pop back open. Steve grinned to himself and kept talking to her until she fell into a deep sleep.

As soon as Steve kissed Virgil on the forehead and got off the bed. Salima knocked on the door. Steve opened it and gestured for him not to disturb Virgil.

"Are you still coming to rehearsal?" Salima asked.

"I guess I am," said Steve in a low voice.

"Looks like she is going to be asleep for a while," said Salima.

"She said she didn't sleep much on the plane."

"That means we can get in the long practice that we should've had all week," said Salima.

"Might as well because it looks like that jet lag is tearing my baby up, she has no idea what country she's in right about now."

Twelve hours later, when Virgil awoke, it was dark outside. Looking over to her side, she saw Steve sound asleep next to her in the moonlight.

'How long have I been asleep?' she thought, looking around for a clock. She spotted Steve's watch on the dresser in the corner. Putting it up to the light, it read a quarter to five.

'Gosh, I've been asleep a long time,' she thought as she sat up and looked down at Steve, wondering whether to wake him or let him sleep. 'I'll let him sleep a little while longer because he probably just got in,' she continued to think to herself.

But, Virgil was getting bored so she moved closer to him, and begin to play with his hair, he didn't wake up. She made little designs on his back, but he still didn't wake up, so she laid on top of him with only a thin sheet between them. Steve opened his eyes.

"Look who decided to rejoin the rest of the world," said Steve.

"I'm still tired."

"So what are you doing up then?"

"I don't know, something just told me to get up. And that's why I'm up? I thought I'd wake up one part of you, and the other half would just follow the leader."

"Are you trying to seduce me?"

"Only if you want to be seduced," Virgil, gave him a little peck on the cheek.

"You can do better than that," said Steve.

Virgil gave him a full kiss on the mouth. "Is that better?"

"Much better, I've seen dogs that get better kisses than that first one."

"Ha! Ha!" said Virgil.

"I've been thinking about making love to you, ever since I found out that you were coming," said Steve.

"You weren't supposed to know."

"Are you crazy, Virgil? I wasn't going to let you just run all over Africa looking for me by yourself."

"Let's not talk anymore," Virgil removed the sheet that separated them. She replaced herself on top of Steve and started to rub her pearl tongue over Steve's manhood.

Steve kissed her deeply, rubbing his hands all over her soft skin, gripping her firm buttocks. Raising her up a little, he put both nipples in his mouth at the same time. This felt really good to Virgil and she began to move faster and pump harder.

Steve continued to nibble on both nipples.

"Move with me," Virgil, gripped the sheets, preparing for a smooth landing, Steve began to work with her, putting his arms around her slender body and pressing her closer, while his baby maker played with her clit in between.

"Oh, Steve," Virgil whispered, "come with me."

Steve's cock stiffened as they moved together. You could hear the sounds of Virgil's juices as they went on screwing each other without Steve even entering Virgil's cave.

"I'm getting ready to come, baby," said Virgil.

Don't wait for me. "I'll be right behind you."

Virgil almost bent her nails back, as she gripped the sheets, letting spurts of cum escape her body. She kept moving afterwards, letting Steve come on her pubic hairs and lower stomach.

Virgil spread the cum all over her breasts like jelly and licked her fingers clean. They then laid in each other's arms and fell asleep.

It was two o'clock in the afternoon when Steve rolled over, reaching for Virgil but just finding an empty spot instead. Virgil came strutting out of the bathroom with a bright red bathing suit on, sandals, sunglasses, and a sheersun robe.

"Virgil, where are you going?"

"Swimming, and so are you." She removed the thin covers off of him, revealing his nakedness.

"I thought we'd just stay in bed all day."

"Now, that sounds like a good idea. It really does, but right now I want to take a dip in some nice cool water." Virgil pulled Steve out of bed and pushed him in the direction of the bathroom.

"Oh all right, I guess a little water won't hurt," said Steve. When Steve was ready to go. He and Virgil found the hotel pool and raced to jump in.

"Now isn't this fun?" Virgil splashed water in Steve's face.

"You're going to pay for that!" Steve picked her up and dropped her into the water.

"That wasn't fair," said Virgil, splashing more water in Steve's face.

"Yes, it was," Steve picked her up higher and dropped her in again.

"Okay, that's enough of that," said Virgil, rubbing her eyes. "Let's swim."

Virgil let Steve take off first, then quickly swam up behind him and pulled his swimming trunks down to his ankles. Before Steve knew what was going on, his shorts were nowhere to be found.

"Now we're even," said Virgil. Swimming back to the edge of the pool while Steve on the other hand, had to go under looking for his trunks.

Steve was underwater a long time and Virgil was beginning to worry until she felt someone trying to pull down the bottom to her bathing suit.

"No! No!" she screamed and quickly got out of the water. Steve jumped out behind her and was having a good laugh.

"I'm going to get you," said Steve. Virgil ran for the elevator with Steve right on her trail. They continued to run past the front desk.

"There will be no running in the hotel," yelled the desk clerk. But, Virgil and Steve kept running until they reached the elevator, kissing and caressing each other wildly as soon as the elevator door closed.

When the door to the elevator opened Steve and Virgil raced to their room. Virgil managed to find the key to the door and Steve slammed the door hard behind him and locked it.

Once inside he took off Virgil's bathing suit and laid her on the massage table by the window and began to spank her with his hard dick. "You've been a bad girl," Steve, made contact with her ass and his dick several times.

"Turn over and open your legs," he ordered. Steve beat his meat against Virgil's pearl tongue and love hole. "Now, why were you mean to me?" said Steve loudly. Virgil didn't answer. "Answer me, girl."

"I was sick," replied Virgil.

"Sick? Then you will have to have a thorough examination," he said, enjoying their role-playing.

"Now where do you feel sick?"

"All over."

Steve first began at the top, looking into Virgil's ears with a small flashlight. "Let's see, there doesn't seem to be a problem here, but I better make sure." Steve stuck his tongue into Virgil's ear, moving it all about for a few seconds, then removed it.

"That's great, Doctor. Can you do that again?"

"I don't have the time today, sweetie. I have other patients you know." Steve then searched Virgil's mouth. "There doesn't seem to be a problem here either, but I'd better make sure. Stick out your tongue."

Virgil obeyed. Steve slapped his dick on Virgil's tongue and began to move it in and out.

Steve was getting the hang of his doctor role. "Somebody give me strength, because that was perfect. Okay, now put your knees up and open your legs wide," Steve looked at Virgil's clit through a microscope.

He played with it, licked it a few times, and came to the conclusion that it there wasn't anything wrong with it. "Now, that's a nice hole." Steve stuck two fingers into Virgil's twat and poked around in there to see what was going on.

"I didn't seem to find anything wrong inside, but I have to make sure, so you better brace yourself."

Virgil gripped the bottom of the table with both hands. Steve stuck his dick in and moved it into every position possible.

"Ah!" exclaimed Steve. He removed himself from Virgil's hole and paused as if to be thinking about something. "Let me double-check this one to make sure." Steve poked around a little bit more before pulling out his dick with Virgil's juices all over it.

"Did you find anything?" asked Virgil.

"No, not exactly, but you seem to have a terrible leak though. There is one more thing that I need to check, so I will need you to turn over and get on your knees. Sticking your ass towards the ceiling.

Again, Virgil obeyed. Steve got on his knees behind her, stuck two fingers in first to find Virgil's anus juices flowing. "There seems to be something wrong inside, I'm going to have to go in.

Take a deep breath," Steve carefully put his dick in, poking about inside Virgil's anus until it began to loosen up. "How's that?"

"Fine, I'm beginning to feel better already," said Virgil, rubbing on her clit, making her pussy nice and wet.

"This is going to take longer than I thought," said Steve with his eyes rolling in the back of his head as he gently fucked Virgil's shit hole. Virgil turned to watch Steve's dick go in and out, this always seems to turn her on more.

"Ooohh," she moaned, licking her fingers from the juices of her neglected cunt.

"Let me have it. I want you to come all over my ass."

Steve gradually picked up full speed, with his nuts slapping against her.

"Come on my ass, let it drip on my ass."

Steve's shot cum all over Virgil's ass just like she wanted it. After smoothing some over her hot cheeks, she spread the rest between her legs then licked her fingers clean.

After they were finished. Steve handed Virgil two pieces of paper. "Here's your prescription and here's your appointment. I need to see you back here later on for a follow-up."

"Yes, doctor," Virgil replied, before heading to the bathroom to soak her aching asshole. Sinking down in the warm water with Steve taking his place behind her, she rested her head on his chest, and they just relaxed in the warm bubbly water for a bit without uttering a word.

Steve was the first to break the silence. "I'm glad you're here."

"I'm glad to be here," said Virgil.

"How long do you think we should stay in this tub?" asked Steve, getting very comfortable.

"Oh, I don't know," said Virgil, "until my ass feels better." They laughed.

"We shouldn't stay in too long. We might fall asleep and drown," said Steve.

"Speak for yourself. I'm tired, but I couldn't fall asleep with this pain in my ass."

"I'm sorry. Do you want me to kiss it and make it all better again?"

"If you want, but it will be fine. I just have to get used to it again, since we don't do that one too often."

"Okay, since you're the one in pain, I'll wash you first and then you can wash me afterwards."

"Sounds good," said Virgil.

A week later Virgil went with Steve to rehearsal. She wasn't pleased with her initial look at the place. She was expecting more.

"Is this where you guys practice?"

"Yes, is there a problem?" asked Steve.

"No, it's just that the only thing in here is three big fans, equipment, a glass room, and four walls."

Steve waved his hands around the room. "This is all the room that we need."

"Okay, okay, you don't have to get jumpy." "So what do you want me to do while you guys practice?"

"Nothing, just watch and listen, or you can read or write postcards. When the other guys get here, I'll introduce you to them, and we'll try to finish as soon as possible so I can take my favorite girl out to dinner."

"Take your time, honey, I'll be fine."

"Sure you will, until you get bored and walk off somewhere, then I'll have to come looking for you."

Virgil mumbled under her breath. "No, I won't. I'll be here the entire time because I have nowhere else to go."

"What did you say?" asked Steve. "I heard that. Virgil, if you feel yourself getting bored and we're at a pause or break, just raise your hand. I'll come from behind that glass and I'll call it quits for today and tell everyone that my baby is getting restless."

Virgil raised both of her hands high. "Okay, I can do that."

Steve gave her a little squeeze. "Silly girl."

Practice wasn't as bad as Virgil thought it would be. Keair was late as usual and they started without him as usual. But other than that, there were very few mistakes, and Steve continued their evening as planned.

Steve surprised Virgil by taking her to a high class restaurant on the other side of the city from the Village in which they were staying. As soon as Steve pushed Virgil's chair under her at the table. A waiter came over with a bouquet of flowers and handed them to her.

Virgil looked at Steve with a warm smile. "Thank you, Steve, these are lovely," Virgil stuck her nose deep into the flowers and smelled them.

Steve looked surprised. "I didn't get those for you. Maybe your boyfriend sent them."

Virgil thought about Pedro. "No way! You gave them to me. Now stop joking around."

"Yes, I gave them to you," Steve got out of his chair and gave her a sloppy kiss on the cheek.

'Thank heaven,' Virgil thought to herself. 'He had me going for a minute.'

"How are things back home?"

"Everything is fine."

"What about Liza?"

"The same," said Virgil with a grin. "She's never going to change, even you know that."

"When is she going to tie the knot with John and have a baby?"

"Now that's a good question," replied Virgil. "I don't have the answer to that one."

"I don't think anyone does." said Steve.

Virgil laughed. "Do you know, she told me that I couldn't come over here?"

"Why did she say that to you?"

"Because she couldn't come."

"She should have came, no one was stopping her."

"John wasn't going to let Liza come alone."

"He could've came too."

"No way, and miss one of his business trips? Besides, he wouldn't let her come here by herself and get buck wild with the jungle boys. He knows how she is."

Virgil and Steve didn't have to wait long before the waiter came back with their dinner.

Virgil eyes widened as the waiter arrived with the platters of food.

"Dinner is served," said Virgil rubbing her hands eagerly together.

"That looks good," Steve bent down and took a long sniff across his dinner. "I'm going to enjoy this."

Virgil and Steve ate their food in silence.

After they were done eating, the waiter came over to check on them.

"Would you like some more wine?" he asked with a big smile.

"Why, sure," Virgil, gave him a big smile back.

"Are you flirting with that waiter?"

"No, no, I'm not flirting," Virgil took a sip of her wine and she and Steve spent hours after dinner just talking about old times.

After they left the resturant, they went for a walk. Virgil you're quiet this evening. Is something bothering you? Or do you have any questions for me?"

"Yes, I do. Only one. I just want to know if you are still going to make good on your promise?"

"What promise?"

"You know, the one that you made to April and I when we were in her room."

"Yes, I meant what I said. It will be so wonderful to go back to my own home again" said Steve.

"I went there one night and looked inside the refrigerator and there weren't any snacks" said Virgil.

"No one told you to leave." said Steve.

"I know, but it's so lonely there without you, so I go over to Mom and Dad's house. There's always something to eat over there."

"You're right. It does get kind of lonely when we're away from each other, although I have the band to cheer me up when things get rough, but it's still not the same." Steve put his arm around Virgil's neck.

There was another person that also kept my spirit alive. "When I first got here, I met this little African boy. He's very poor, but also very smart. Sometimes you feel so sorry for some of them, but there's no way that you can help them all.

Anyway, the boy that I met. His name is, Ja . . . his name is, Jahim . . . I'm not good with those names, but I was thinking about getting him checked out and bring him back to the States with us. I thought maybe your father or I could give him a job.

He's entirely too smart to be in the position that he is in," explained Steve. "So what do you think?"

"If you think that he's okay, then I'm sure that my father wouldn't mind I know my mother would just spoil him rotten no matter what."

"What about your feelings, your true feelings?" Steve asked.

"How old is this boy?"

"Thirteen," said Steve.

"Thirteen," Virgil repeated. "He's young."

"You won't have to look after him, we can hire someone. We'll pay Charles and Rose extra to look after him. He's very intelligent, and he catches on really fast. I'm sure he won't be too much of a bother.

"We can hire him a private tutor to see where he is on the American level, and then we will take it from there. We have the money, so now, it's time to give back to those less fortunate than we are."

"You're right, we do have the money. So when do I meet him?"

"Tomorrow evening. Someone has to bring him to us because, it's not safe for us to go to him."

Virgil put her arm around Steve's waist.

"We have sixteen days left, Steve. What are we going to do with them?" asked Virgil. "I was thinking about taking some pictures of giraffes, monkeys, and big old elephants to show April when we get back home."

"I'll spend a couple of days with Jahim so he won't be a complete stranger to us, stay in bed all day, go swimming, and stay in bed all day, then all day again."

"Sounds like you have a one-track mind." "But it is a good idea." Laughed Steve.

For the next few days, Virgil spent all of her free time with Jahim, while Steve worked. They had picnics, played some of his games, and did plenty of shopping in Virgil's honor. Virgil began to enjoy being around Jahim.

'Steve's right, he is a smart kid,' Virgil thought, as she watched Jahim draw a picture of their day in the sand.

One evening when Steve and Virgil were relaxing. "Gosh, time sure does fly when you're having fun," said Virgil. "We only have a couple of days left."

"You're right, the last few days went by very fast," said Steve.

"Did you get all the paperwork done?" asked Virgil.

"Yes, everything went smoothly. Jahim is in perfect health except for a few cavities and a minor cold. I also have permission to take him now if I want, but I think that he should spend his remaining time with his real family, before I take him away."

"You are a kind man Steve. That's why I love you so much," said Virgil. "Have you ever talked to his mother?"

"No, but I heard that she wants him to go so that he can be taken care of, but that's only what I've heard."

"Could you arrange for me to meet with her?"

"I probably could, I'll see what I can do. Now remember, she doesn't speak English. I'll have to arrange for an interpreter and some body guards."

"Tell me about them," said Virgil.

"Well, the father died sometime ago of a heart attack, leaving the mother behind with three kids and a mother-in-law."

"I'll feel much more comfortable if I talk with her to get her own personal feelings about Jahim leaving. He's the man of the house now."

"Since you feel that deeply about it, I'll make sure that you meet with her."

The next day Virgil was able to meet with Jahim's mother and family. A reliable source made it all possible. They were driven several miles away to a tiny village and the meeting was successful.

When Virgil and Steve left out of the small hut and rode back to their hotel, Virgil felt relieved about taking Jahim back to the United States.

They entered their hotel room and Virgil sat quietly on the bed.

Steve walked over and sat down on the bed beside her. "What's the matter, honey?"

"Oh, I'll be alright I'm just thinking about Jahim's family, I feel so sorry for them I just wanted to make sure that I met with his mother to get her true feeling about all of this."

"But the one thing that she said that stood out and I'll never forget is: 'My boy is the reason that we are all living today, but if it means the key to his freedom and happiness, then we will manage the best way we can and may the Lord be with us.'"

Two day later Virgil, Jahim, and Steve were on the plane back to the U. S. Virgil spent her time sleeping while Steve stayed up with Jahim, who was very fascinated by all the strange faces and the not—so—smooth plane ride, especially the air pockets. The only word that he could say about that was "crash."

Steve looked at Jahim and smiled. "No, no, it's only the wind and the clouds," Steve said as he tried to explain to Jahim in a way that he'd understand without him asking a lot of questions.

Jahim looked around the cabin, of the plane and noticed that no one else had panicked, so he relaxed and decided it would be less nerve-wracking if he'd just fall asleep.

After many hours of sleep. Virgil woke up and looked out of the plane's window.

"Jahim! Jahim, wake up!" Virgil, shook the poor boy wildly. Jahim slowly opened his eyes. "Look," said Virgil, pointing down below.

"City!" cried Jahim.

"Big city!" Jahim repeated. Steve and Virgil smiled. They also had a hard time keeping up with him once they were inside of the airport terminal. Jahim kept running around, touching things, speaking to everyone and also introducing himself to everyone.

While they waited for their luggage, Virgil had to stand guard, holding Jahim by the arm while Steve got the luggage. After the luggage was loaded into the limo, they decided to give Jahim a tour of the city before they headed home, since he was so wired up.

They bought him clothes, shoes, toys, and anything else that he wanted. Steve and Virgil thought that Jahim was never going to get tired. Luckily for Steve's wallet, the shopping center closed at nine.

Jahim fell asleep in the limo on the way home. The limo pulled up into the driveway of Steve and Virgil's home.

Virgil looked down at Jahim. "What do you think we should do?" asked Virgil. "I think that we should start that boy to work right away. If he had one more hour, he would've maxed out my credit cards!"

"Steve, you can always go get more money," said Virgil, giving him a little slap on the arm. "And besides, I was asking you about where do you want Jahim to sleep tonight."

"Oh, I think that he should spend the night at our house first, so that he won't wake up to a bunch of strange faces in the morning," Steve, lifted Jahim out of the back seat.

The chauffeur opened the door and Steve struggled to get Jahim out of the car.

"Looks like you're having a hard time with him," said Virgil, with a small grin.

"I am," said Steve. "This boy is small but heavy."

"Don't blame it on the boy, you probably need to go to the gym."

"Are you trying to say that I'm out of shape?" asked Steve. "I will show you who's out of shape as soon as I get him tucked in."

"I think that you're all talk." Virgil opened the door to an extra room where Steve tucked in Jahim, leaving a small lamp on in case he got up in the middle of the night.

Virgil also wrote the word for restroom on some index cards, and taped them to the floor all the way to the bathroom. "There shouldn't be any problems now," she said. Since Jahim was used to that word.

When Virgil was done, Steve turned to face her. "Now, what was it that you were saying about ten minutes ago?"

"I haven't the foggiest idea what you are talking about," said Virgil.

"Oh, I'll make you remember. As for now, you're my prisoner, so come on downstairs with me. I have something to show you."

Virgil stopped in place. "I don't have to go anywhere that I don't want to."

Steve reached inside of a drawer, took out some hand cuffs, and slapped them on her wrist. "Now like I said, march your big ass downstairs," ordered Steve.

In the family room, there was an oversized couch and love seat, a big screen T.V., a pool table in the corner area, a wet bar and other amenities . . . Steve selected an X-rated movie from the video cabinet with his eyes closed and put it in the DVD.

"I don't know what's on this movie, but whatever it is, we are going to do whatever they're doing."

Steve and Virgil watched the movie for awhile before Steve started to get uncomfortable and begin to take off his pants and shirt, leaving on just his underwear.

He also removed Virgil's pants, leaving her with an open blouse, no bra, and G-string bikini panties. He then put his hand into his underwear and begin to play with his dick.

After a few minutes. He thought that he would check Virgil's panties for wetness. They felt moist from the outside. "Time's up." Steve, turned off the T.V. and the DVD. "I'll be right back."

Virgil stretched out on the couch with her handcuffed hands over her head and her legs rested up against the back of the couch. Steve soon returned with a basket of bananas, whipped cream, and strawberries, that Charles had gotten from the store earlier.

He took a small empty bowl off the coffee table and put some whipped cream in it along with a few strawberries. He rolled one strawberry around in the cream, he took one bite, then put the rest into Virgil's mouth.

He then pushed her blouse aside to expose her nipples, decorated them both with whipped cream and sucked them clean. After removing her panties, He started from the top of her lips and squeezed a narrow line of whipped cream straight down to her eternal sex drive.

He then licked the cream nice and slow, making Virgil arch her back when he nibbled the whipped cream off her clit. Reaching for the banana, he also covered it with whipped cream.

He squeezed a little at the entrance of her eager hole and eased it in.

To Virgil, this banana wasn't like any ordinary banana. This banana was big and firm and felt like a real dick. Steve continued to slide the banana in and out until he put it all the way in and then took it out again.

Steve also got his thrill on by watching how Virgil's pussy gripped the banana and by the way she lifted her hips to fuck her fake replacement. After a while, Steve covered Virgil's clit with whipped cream and began to nibble at it while he increased the pace of the banana.

Virgil tossed her head from side to side like she always did when something felt good to her. She begin to throw her hips harder at the banana, so hard that Steve thought he was going to lose his grip.

Virgil was having too much fun, and Steve couldn't take it anymore. He took out the banana and yanked off his underwear.

He picked up a smaller banana, covered it with cream, put it in her Vagina halfway, with his dick alongside it, and begin to hump her with the thrill of having two cocks inside of the same hole.

Virgil and Steve screamed together as their mixtures of cum dripped all over the banana and down Virgil's thighs. Virgil caressed Steve's hard ass while he laid still on top of her. Soon the banana began to ease out. Steve tossed it aside.

Sliding his hands under Virgil's ass, he gave one final push and exploded once more into her warm snatch.

Less than a minute later, Virgil began to hear a little snore from Steve. "Honey, honey." Virgil tapped him gently on the buttocks. "We can't sleep here."

"Why not?" asked Steve.

"Do you remember what happened last time?"

"Oh, how can I forget? Rose had only been working here a month. She came in here and saw us laying next to each other naked, just like this. I saw her and panicked. And I hopped off the couch, and my dick was hard again.

Her eyes got big, and she just stood there, not moving a single muscle. You called her name after I left, but she wouldn't respond. Charles had to sit her down, put water on her face, and fan her back to normal," said Steve, laughing a little.

"I'll never forget the look on her face."

"Good, now if you don't want to see that look again, we better get to climbing those stairs to our own room."

Virgil and Steve quickly got dressed and and went upstairs. They slowly entered into the extra room where Jahim was sleeping to check on him. "I don't think that he's going to get up just yet," said Virgil.

"That jet lag has struck again," said Steve, pulling the covers up to Jahim's shoulders. "I think that we should get some shut-eye also, because when your family catches wind that we're home, it's going to be lack of sleep for all of us."

"Watch how you talk about my family," said Virgil, slapping Steve on the buttock as she followed him to their bedroom.

"Okay, Virgil, let's play a little game. If you can make it to the room first and be buck naked before me, I won't hit you back, and I'll do all the explaining to your parents as to why we didn't tell them that we're home."

Virgil took off running towards their room ripping off her clothes in the process. She made it to the bed first, without her clothes, and Steve was right behind her with a homerun on top of her.

"Mmm, now this is living," said Steve, giving her a full kiss.

After Virgil got really comfortable and Steve was asleep, she suddenly realized that they'd left the banana's and the whipped cream in the family room.

"Ah shit!" said Virgil to herself as she grabbed her robe and ran downstairs. Upon reaching the family room, Virgil saw Charles watching the movie that they started. He was eating the strawberries with whipped cream.

The two bananas were sticking out from under a pillow.

"Oh no," she said to herself, standing on the outside of the room, trying to figure out what to do. Virgil finally decided to crawl to the back of the couch since Charles was in the recliner with his back to the her.

Virgil peeked around the couch to make sure that Charles was still watching the movie before she jumped up and grabbed one of the bananas. She waited a little while, checked again, then grabbed the other one.

She was just beginning to prepare for another peek around the corner when Charles got up from the recliner and pounced on the couch in front of her. He then unzipped his pants.

"Mmmm," he groaned.

Virgil swallowed hard, 'that's not good. Now, what am I to do?' she thought.

"Swing that ass," said Charles, as he began to jack off.

"Oohh, I wish I had that pussy on my dick right now," he murmured. Charles was having a great time.

Virgil, on the other hand, decided to stay for the show. She moved over to the end of the couch to watch Charles beat his huge meat.

"Look at those lips, come and suck my dick like that," he said.

Virgil began to grow horny. She wanted to jump on top of Charles and fuck him. But instead, she just slowly left out the same way that she'd came in.

'We've got to stop being so sloppy,' Virgil thought, pulling off her robe and climbing into bed, moving as close as she could behind Steve, so close that her clit touched his butt cheeks, and that's how she fell asleep.

Chapter 8

Steve peeked into Jahim's room and found Virgil's mom and dad already in there. "So you couldn't wait until we made it to your house?" he asked, walking into the room to find Virgil's whole family in there.

"Ana called Rose this morning Rose told Ana and Ana told us," said Mom.

"So you rushed right over?" said Steve.

"Wouldn't miss it," said Mom.

"Give us a break," said Dad.

"Okay, I'm sorry." You guys must be really excited, especially when we didn't tell you that we were bringing a guest—a permanent guest."

"Let's go into the study. You can tell me all about it," said Dad.

Just then Virgil ran down the hall towards Jahim's room. "What's all the commotion about? Virgil turned towards Jahim. Did these people frighten you?"

"No, Mommy Virgil, they good."

Liza pushed Virgil. "Watch it, if anyone should be frightened, it's all of us. Looking at you first thing in the morning is a very scary thing to experience," said Liza. Everyone laughed, including April who doesn't even know what she was laughing at.

Virgil picked April up. "Do you think Mommy looks funny? You better say no, or I'm not going to give you all of the presents I brought you," said Virgil. April laughed again.

"You naughty girl, it's not nice to make fun of your mama," said Virgil in her pretend baby talk.

Meanwhile, in the study . . . .

"So what do you think of Jahim?" Steve asked his father-in-law.

"He seems to be a strong boy, a little lean but that's only temporary. I was thinking about starting him in with the horses. I'll explain to him that this is a job and he's getting paid with money for what he's doing.

"Since he's from a different country and his understanding is a little delayed, I think that we should have a tutor brought in to teach him what he doesn't know. But for now, I think that we should let him get adjusted to just being a kid before we teach him the ropes," Dad added.

"Is it okay for us to keep a room for him, because you know how you and Mom are," said Steve.

"Sure, go for it, we're going to share our time with him, we will come up with some kind of schedule or something."

"Then he'll know that he is truly important, with three homes and three families."

"Oh, one more thing. Your mother and I want to spend the day with Jahim, just to get to know him better and for him to get used to us."

"Make sure that you take him to the car store because he loves cars."

"Is it the one on Madison?" asked Dad.

"No, the real car store, the one on Jackson."

"Oh boy, he just got here and wants to drive already?" Dad chuckled as he walked out the door.

Steve laughed. "Have a nice day with Jahim, Dad, and bring plenty of money, you're going to need it."

Later on that night Steve was a little irritated because Virgil's parents did not bring the kids back as promised.

"I don't know about your family, it's eleven o'clock at night, and your parent's haven't brought neither one of the kids back here yet."

"And if you know them like I know them, they're not bringin' them back either," said Virgil. "I'm turning them in for child snatching.

'I spent all of two hours with April today before your mom comes running in and explained to me how she has to take pictures of Jahim and April together. 'They have to get used to one another,' she said.

"Oh, honey, you know how my mother is. Since you're going to be spending more time around the house, you'll get to see April on a regular basic or get smarter than my mother," Virgil grinned.

"I think I'll go over there bright and early in the morning and pick them up."

"Now that, that's settled, come and take a dip in the pool with me," said Virgil.

Virgil made it to the pool first and removed all of her clothes Steve dove in after her, pretending to be a sea monster and tried to attack her. They played around for hours until Steve decided that he was tired.

"I'm going in, this chlorine is irritating my eyes."

"Are you going to be all right out here by yourself?"

"I'll be fine," said Virgil.

"Don't be too long," said Steve.

"Okay," Virgil replied. When Virgil was alone she made circles, stood on her hands, and pretended that Steve was still chasing her until she got bored and also decided to turn in. Gathering up her clothes, she decided not to get dressed.

She covered herself with a towel and was about to open the rear sliding door when someone put their hand over her mouth and forced her against the wall.

"Hi, Virgil," said Pedro.

"Pedro!" exclaimed Virgil as her words muffled beneath his hand.

"You recognized me?" asked Pedro. He removed his hand from her mouth.

"I thought that you quit."

"I was going to until I heard that you were coming back, so I changed my mind," Pedro, moved a little closer to Virgil, pressing everything that he had against her.

Virgil could feel his hardness through the wet towel. "You didn't tell Steve about us, did you?"

"Now, why would I do a stupid thing like that?" said Virgil.

"Because I read it in your book, Steve and I tell each other everything," said Pedro sarcastically.

"Well, I didn't tell him that one."

"Good, because I really like my job and I don't want your husband telling your dad to get rid of me." Pedro stared into Virgil's eyes, and unwrapped Virgil's towel. "You know, I kind of missed you while you were away."

"I have to go," Virgil, grabbed her towel and ran into the house.

That night, Virgil began to dream about Pedro. She dreamed that he was fucking her like never before, grinding his shaft in and out of her and spurting his cum all over her face and mouth.

She awoke quickly with a chill running down her spine and a deep craving for Pedro. She looked around the room, but no one was there except her and Steve.

"Shit," said Virgil, wiping the perspiration from her forehead. She got out of bed and walked to the balcony. Peeking out of the curtains, she saw Pedro's light on. 'Should I go to him?' she asked herself. She then turned around to look at Steve who was now snoring.

She soon changed her mind and went back to bed, but she couldn't sleep though, her pussy was throbbing for Pedro to come and take her like he'd already once done.

Virgil finally fell asleep and was only a sleep for what seemed like a short period of time, when Steve woke her up and open the curtains.

"Honey, did you sleep good last night?" he asked.

"Yes, why do you ask?"

"Because you kept tossing and turning."

"No, I slept okay, except for a small bad dream. I awoke from it, got something to drink, got back into bed, then I was okay."

"What was it about?" asked Steve.

"I don't know, some monster was trying to get me. I don't know what it meant though, I've heard if you dream something, there's a reason for it," explained Virgil.

"The next time that a monster comes after you, you just call me."

"Okay." said Virgil.

"Let's do something different today. Let's go horseback riding." said Steve.

"Sounds good," said Virgil.

"I'll go get dress and meet you downstairs for breakfast because I know that it'll take you longer to find something to wear."

"Whatever," said Virgil.

Virgil and Steve had a light breakfast, then hurried to the stables to saddled up the horses.

"Now, I have a hundred dollars that says your horse can't beat my horse down to the river," said Steve. Virgil took off first like always.

"You're a cheater!" yelled Steve as he caught up with her and passed her up, reaching the river bank first.

"It's about time that you got here, I was about to get worried," he said.

"Very funny," said Virgil.

"I want my money," Steve, held out his hand for payment. "I also want an extra hundred dollars."

"Why is that?" asked Virgil.

"Because you tried to cheat."

Virgil got off of her horse and pulled both horses under a nice big shady tree. She then tied her horse to that tree, and removed her clothes and hopped up into the saddle facing Steve.

"I have an ideal, I'll let you give me a little ride around these big trees a couple of times, and we can call it even."

"What if I don't want to give you a ride?"

"Then I'll give you one," said Virgil, turning around on the horse so that her ass stuck out towards Steve.

Virgil told Steve's horse to break out into a little trot. Steve watched as Virgil's ass went back and forth on the saddle, making his cock swell. Virgil didn't think her plan was working fast enough so she leaned over to give him a better view.

Steve began to rub his rock-hard penis, which was trying desperately to escape from his pants. He freed it and moved closer to Virgil so that when her ass flopped down, it touched his dick.

After a while, Steve's precum juices began to flow, letting him know that this teasing game wasn't going to cut it. He braced himself and slipped his wet head and dick body into Virgil's already wet slit.

It wasn't long before Virgil and Steve fucked with the rhythm of the horse's trot. Virgil held on tight as Steve rubbed his hands all over her body, caressing her nipples and pulling back her ass cheeks to guide himself inside of her.

Virgil moaned loudly and urged the horse to go a little faster. It took Steve only a minute to catch up with the horse's gallop and sent Virgil's ass cheeks into a half wave, every time his body impacted with hers.

Virgil continued to moan as Steve tingled the insides of her pussy. Leaning back, letting her skin touch his skin, she put one arm around his neck and began to kiss him fully while he squeezed the softness of her breast and the hardness of her nipples.

Moving his hands down to her clit, he then began to finger it, causing Virgil to move helplessly in the saddle. Steve moved with her, without removing his fingers, causing her juices to run on to the saddle.

Feeling the increase of juice on his fingers, Steve began to bang his body hard against hers.

Virgil's neck began to ache. She returned to her regular position and that's what Steve was waiting for. "Hold on," he said as he began to pump Virgil so fast that the horse lost track and stopped trotting.

But Steve didn't stop. He had gotten so confident up on that horse that he held the back of the saddle and was, so deep inside of her that it felt like he was cleaning off Virgil's ribs with his dick.

Virgil sent screams of pleasure echoing through the air, but one final push sent them both into an erotic orgasm.

After holding each other and resting on the horse for a minute or two. Steve and Virgil climb down off the horse and dressed slowly. Steve trotted his confused horse back to the stables, while Virgil followed at a slower pace.

"You know, Steve, I really have to take a bath. I smell just like your horse."

"Well, what do you expect, carrying on the way that you did today."

"You didn't seem to mind."

"I didn't have much choice."

"You could have turned the other cheek."

"And miss all of that good wet pussy? I don't think so, but I do know one thing. My dick hurts from fucking you so much, so you won't get any tonight."

"What if I take it?"

"Then I'll scream rape. Rose will come in and save me."

Virgil burst out laughing. "Save your screams, I'm a little sore myself. We should call it a rest for a while."

"Let's go and take a nice long shower," said Steve. "After that, you're going over to Mom's and take April for a little stroll and I'm going to take Jahim for that horseback ride that he's been asking me about. But this time, I think we'll take your horse. Mine is a little worn out right now."

"After I take April for her stroll, I'm going to the gym and do some working out."

"Now, honey, even I know that you're not going to do any exercising. You and Liza are just going there to look at the men's bodies."

"That's not true. Why don't you come with us and see for yourself?"

"That's okay, I'm going to stay here with the kids where it doesn't require any more workout."

"Whimp," said Virgil.

"Excuse me, but does it look like I need to go to the gym?" Steve pulled off his shirt and posed for her.

"I don't need to go either, but you will never know when fat and old age might sneak up on you. Beware, beware," said Virgil in a creepy voice as she tickled Steve's stomach.

"Cut it out, that tickles."

"Okay, okay. Are you sure that you don't want to come to the gym with me?"

"Where are you working out at?"

"I'm going to the "Sprint Club" over by Liza's."

"I'll take a rain check. I really want to spend sometime with the kids before your parents come and claw them away again. I'll catch up with you later at dinner," Steve, gave Virgil a big kiss. "Thanks for today.

That was a new one. We'll have to do that again sometime."

Virgil laughed. "But not too soon."

Chapter 9

Liza made it to the gym before Virgil as always.

She found Liza pretending to stretch her legs over by the running machines.

"I thought that I would find you here," said Virgil.

"You know it. Why are you late anyway?"

"I got held up."

"Held up how?" asked Liza.

"You wouldn't believe me if I told you."

"I probably wouldn't, but tell me anyway."

"It's like this, this afternoon Steve and I made love on his horse and that's the whole story."

Liza looked at Virgil. "They make beds for that, you know, windows that close, and I might as well add, doors that lock—it's called privacy."

"You know, your imagination is very limited. You should try it sometime instead of knocking it all of the time. Believe me, it was worth the ride."

"John and I do some pretty weird things, but nothing compared to you and Steve. You guys are crazy! Now give me details."

"I don't believe you. You always have something smart to say about what we do, and in the end, you always want to know every single detail."

"Is there something wrong with sharing intimate thoughts with your sis?"

"No, but you should get your own gossip."

"Oh please, John is a house and car man. If we're not in one place, we're definitely in the other. I'm kind of tired of fucking in just two places, with the exception of that time at the pool, and it had to have been the wine. Other than that, it gets pretty old."

"Speaking of pools, Steve and I went skinny-dipping the night before."

"See what I mean? You guys have all the fun."

"No, wait, Steve got out before me. I stayed in for a little while longer. After swimming around for a couple of hours by myself, I grew tired and got out. I was walking to the house with the towel around me, my clothes in my hands, and guess who I ran into?"

"No!" said Liza.

"Yes!" Virgil said. "He wanted to fuck me, but I wouldn't let him. I did want to fuck him. But, who does he think he is?

Just because he cleans my pool and my family's pool doesn't mean that he can just pop up whenever he wants. Besides, I think that he's spending more time in my pool house just to get next to me. When before he always stayed in Mom and Dad's pool house."

"So do you think that you are going to be able to undo his spell?"

"I'm sure," said Virgil.

"Just like that?" said Liza. "Do you really think that you can do it while he's still walking around working for you. You're good girl, I wouldn't be able to do it."

"Don't worry, I will figure something out," said Virgil.

Virgil put her finger up to her forehead and quickly removed it. "I just got an idea. Steve and I are doing our fantasy thing, right?" Liza shook her head in agreement.

"We only put it on hold while we were in Africa, so what I need for you to do is to convince Steve to arrange for me to fuck Pedro, while he watches, of course."

"Are you crazy?" said Liza.

"I'm not supposed to know, remember?"

"No one told you to tell him. I just want you to convince Steve to arrange for me to be with Pedro. Tell him that it is a good idea."

"How am I supposed to do that without giving him some kind of hint that I'm aware of what's going on?"

"Liza, listen to me," said Virgil calmly. "All you have to do is talk to him one day, ask him if he met Pedro, and say some nice things about his body. Then say, I think Virgil likes him."

"What if he asks me more about this liking thing?"

"Then that's when you play dumb. You can figure that one out, can't you?"

"Ha! You think you have it all figured out, don't you? Well, I wouldn't get so happy about it yet, Miss Missy. I might just tell him that you want to do it with Mike instead."

"You wouldn't," said Virgil.

"No, probably not, I just wanted to keep you on your toes," explained Liza.

"So when are you going to do it?" asked Virgil, hopping on a exercise bike and began to pedal.

"Why are you in such a rush?" Liza jumped on the bike next to Virgil.

"I'll tell you what," said Virgil.

"Oh boy, here we go again," said Liza.

"Listen, if you do this for me, I'll never mess with him again. I just want one last time with him and after that, Steve and I will finish what we started. I won't ask you to do it again."

"You are breaking the rules. Never fuck them twice," said Liza.

"I know, but I just want to do it one more time. I'll even change the time a little. It doesn't have to be anytime soon, surprise me later on."

"Now that's better, I don't have to rush with a plan. I hate to be rushed," said Liza.

"So does that mean that you'll do it then?"

"I guess so, but you better not get me in any trouble with Steve."

"Great!" screamed Virgil. "Let's celebrate, let's get some ice cream."

"Ice cream?" asked Liza. "We haven't even done a full fifteen minutes yet, and you want to go and get ice cream?"

"Like Steve said today, I don't need to go to the gym, do you?"

"If you put it that way," said Liza, getting off the bike and following Virgil out the door and over to the Ice cream parlor across the street.

"What kind of ice cream do you want?" asked Virgil.

"I want whatever he's having," said Liza, pointing to the guy in the corner eating a vanilla ice cream cone.

"We didn't come here to have sex. We came for ice cream."

"I don't want to fuck him yet, I just want him to lick me like he's doing that ice cream. His tongue is real long too. He probably could lick us both in one lay."

The guy behind the counter stopped and looked at Liza.

"You'll have to excuse my sister. They gave her the wrong medicine this morning and she' having an allergic reaction. The guy behind the counter gave them their vanilla ice cream cones and Virgil paid for them.

"Have a nice day," said Virgil to the cashier as she forced one of the ice cream cones into Liza's hands and pushed her out the door. "I can't take you anywhere. Don't you know how to whisper?"

Virgil and Liza stood outside of the ice cream parlor to finish their ice cream cones. "That guy's eyes almost popped out of his head when you said that thing about the other guy's tongue. He couldn't take his eyes off you after that. He almost gave me the scoop instead of the ice cream," said Virgil, laughing.

When they left the ice cream parlor, Virgil and Liza went to Liza's house and sat on the couch to have their midday gossip session.

"Where's John?" asked Virgil.

"Probably still at work," said Liza frowning.

"Tell him to do what Steve did, take a vacation."

"Yeah right," said Liza.

"You can do it. Just plan a romantic dinner for him before he gets home. Put on your sexiest, most revealing evening gown. Try a new approach for when he first walks in the door, and take it from there."

"What kind of approach?"

"You know, don't just give him a kiss and ask him how his day was. Try something else, fuck him on top of the table or something."

Liza thought for a moment. "I know what I'm going to do, so get out!" She pulled Virgil up off the couch.

"What are you talking about?"

"Just how it sounded. See you later." Liza pushed Virgil out of the door and locked it.

After Virgil was out of the way, Liza immediately began to get things ready quickly before John got home.

As soon as John opened the door and walked in. "Surprise!" Liza walked up to him with a long black silky evening dress with high splits on each side and the pumps to match.

John looked down at his now wrinkled suit that he had on since early morning.

Liza read his mind. "Don't worry about it," Liza, sat him down on the couch and put a glass of wine in his hand. "Dinner will be served shortly." She went into the kitchen and quickly brought the food out to the table.

She then went into the living room, took John's hand, and led him to the table to eat.

"Dinner looks lovely. Let's see . . . what do we have here? There's steak, shrimp, potatoes, corn, and rolls. You out did yourself this time, babe,"

John said, holding Liza's chair for her and pushing it under the table once she was seated.

"You're not leaving me, are you?"

"No, I just wanted to add a little spice to our relationship, by sitting down for once and having a romantic dinner. Just the two of us with candles and all."

"Oh, okay, I just thought I should check."

"It was Virgil's idea, but don't tell her that I took her advice."

"Too bad, I wanted to thank her." John took another look at his food. "This is really lovely."

"You said that already. Now let's say our blessings and eat before our food gets cold."

John was hungry, but he didn't eat too much. He couldn't take his eyes off of Liza's low-cut dress with most of her cleavage hanging out. Liza, didn't eat too much either. She was too excited about her evening that was going all too well.

Suddenly Liza dropped her fork. "Oops!" She bent way over to pick it up. "I'll be back, I have to wash this off."

When Liza came back, she didn't sit in her chair. She went over to John and sat on his lap and began to feed him shrimp.

"I love you," said John.

"I love you too," said Liza. "I also have another surprise for you."

"What's that?" asked John.

"It wouldn't be a surprise if I told you what it was, now would it?" John pulled Liza closer to him and kissed her fully on the lips.

"Oh, oh, let's not forget about my surprise. I made dessert." She pulled away from John's grip.

"Can we eat it later?" asked John, he got up out of his seat and grabbed Liza to sit her on an empty space on the table.

"You have to see the dessert, it's the best I've ever made."

"Well, can I convince you to eat it later?" John took out his big rod and ran it along Liza's crotch.

"I'll make a deal with you then, I'll show you the dessert and you can make up your mind from there."

Liza put a bandanna around John's eyes.

"Honey, why do I have to be blindfolded to see a dessert tray?"

"Because it's a surprise and I'm really proud of it." "Now just shut up and take hold of my hand and follow me." Liza lead John into a nearby bathroom.

"You can take it off now." John took off the bandanna and there in front of him, was one-third of the Roman tub filled with red Jell-O gelatin with little hearts made of whipped cream on top.

"Wow! Where did you get an idea like this?" Was all that John managed to say.

"A friend of mine told me about it a while back, but I was too lazy to try it until it dawned on me that the Jell-O doesn't have to be completely done before you can get in it."

"Get in it?" John repeated.

"Yes, silly. What did you think, that we were going to sit on the floor with our spoons and eat out of the tub? As a matter of fact, you will be the first to try it out."

Liza removed John's clothes, revealing his hard on with the exception of some flab here and there.

John looked at Liza first before he stuck one foot halfway into the gelatin.

"It's kind of cold and I don't want to mess up the little hearts."

"Don't worry about the hearts. We'll warm up the gelatin." Liza removed her dress and got inside the tub in front of John.

John grabbed a whole handfull of gelatin and put it into his mouth.

"This taste good." He then picked up another hand full and rubbed it on the side of Liza's face and sucked it off. Liza, in turn, bent over and began sucking John's sticky cock.

"Mmmmm, your cock is sweet." From that point, John decorated Liza's body with gelatin, while she went to work on his gelatin shaft.

Changing the pace, John scooped up some gelatin with his middle finger and pushed it up Liza's lonely twat. Pulling back his finger, he then licked it shiny and clean.

Every once in a while, Liza would throw some more gelatin on John's dick then go down on him and bob for more apples, while John, on the other hand, continued to smoothed gelatin all over and inside of her body.

"Come here," John, gently raised Liza's head and gave her a slight push down in the tub. Liza supported herself with her elbows while John washed her upper body with his long red tongue.

"I want to fuck you," said John.

"Fuck me then," replied Liza. Liza rose up to get on her knees, but John stopped her.

"No, I want you on your back so I can feel some of the gelatin inside you," commanded John. John's dick went in smoothly. Hitting bottom right away, he immediately went to full speed.

You could loudly hear the sex sounds as they stroked together. All of those juices mixed together was too much for John and he had to switch positions.

"Turn over and put your hands and knees down." "I want you from behind now."

Liza obeyed. John's dick kept slipping as he eagerly tried to put it back in. "Let me try," said Liza, guiding his hot rod into home.

"Ah," cried John. He put one foot by Liza's head, both hands on the sides of the tub and began to fuck her sideways, making Liza come instantly. Liza screamed, but John wasn't finished yet. He helped her stand up.

Cocking one leg on the side of the tub, he continued to torture that G-spot while Liza came again and was screaming for mercy.

He then pushed her onto her stomach, closed her legs, and pumped and pumped until his face tightened as her pussy squeezed out all of his thick semen into her gelatin sea.

For a long while, nobody moved, then John slipped out of her and he relaxed himself with his back against the wall of the tub.

Liza joined him.

"Now that was even better than dinner, not that your dinner was bad, but this was much better."

"I know, I was hoping that it would be everything that I imagined it would be."

"Well, you really used your imagination this time. We haven't had this much fun in months," said John.

"I agree," said Liza.

"I also want to tell you that you're right. I know that I've been working too hard lately, depriving you, all the pleasures of sex between us. I'll try and do better from now on."

"Thanks," said Liza.

"But I do have one more question," said John.

"What is it?"

"Since you thought of everything, did you think about how are we going to get down the hall to the next bathroom and take a shower without messing up this white carpet?"

"No, I didn't think that far ahead."

"Then what should we do?" asked John.

"I know, take a towel and wipe the bottom of yourself all the way down, then go to the other bathroom and get in the shower. I'll join you in a minute."

"Good idea," John, got out of the tub dripping the red gelatin all over the pink bathroom rug and white carpet. He looked back at Liza, waiting for her to scold him. "Oh well, I've been meaning to shampoo them anyway," said Liza.

"That's fine, you earned the liberty to walk on them."

Days had passed and Virgil was wondering why she hadn't seen Liza, so she decided to pay her a visit.

"Where have you been, girl? I haven't seen you lately. I had to come over to your house today and see if you were sick or something. Are you hiding from your sis?"

"John's on vacation," Liza smiled.

"Get out of here!"

"Yes, he is, and we have been spending his vacation time very wisely."

"How?" Virgil, moved closer to make sure that she didn't miss anything.

"Well, we locked ourselves inside the house and had sex in every place except the bed."

"Every place?"

"Every place, especially the Roman tub. I put gelatin in it up to our hip bones and we did the wild thing in it. It was good too, until we got sick to our stomachs from eating so much of that stuff off each other."

Virgil was pleased with Liza. "Doing it in the tub, locking yourselves inside of your house, and convincing John to go on vacation. Sounds like you guys are moving up in the world. That's it I think you've got it, so don't let it pass you by."

"Just think about it," said Liza. "All of this time have passed and all I had to do was cook a big meal, put half-done gelatin inside of the Roman tub just to make him go on vacation." They both laughed.

"I have a question for you," said Virgil. "Now how do you do this gelatin thing again?"

"Get your own gossip," said Liza.

Virgil gave Liza an over-eyed look.

"Okay," said Liza, "but I always wanted to say that. Anyway, just pretend like the tub is a bowl and take it from there, but remember one thing.

Let the gelatin get only halfway done so that you can move around easily inside the tub, and most importantly, make sure that you put down towels trailing to the next bathroom to take a shower so that you won't mess up the carpet. I learned that one at the last minute."

"Oh," said Virgil, "now don't you feel good? You actually told me something I didn't know."

"Yes, I do feel good. For once, I've beaten you at the sex game."

"Don't let your head get too big. So far I do have you beat."

"I'm not worried because after the other night, I feel very confident that I'll catch up with you."

Chapter 10

Steve and Jahim ran by the living room door where Virgil and Liza were sitting. Virgil arched her eyebrows.

"Steve!" she hollered. Steve and Jahim stopped in their tracks, hesitating a moment before they backed up to the entrance to the living room door. Steve and Jahim were wet and dirty from head to toe. Virgil took one look at them.

"What happened?"

Steve looked at Jahim. "Do you want to tell them?"

Jahim shook his head in disagreement.

"Okay, but don't laugh," Steve tried to explain. "Jahim and I were playing this game that he used to play at home. When he names an animal, we have to act and behave like that animal, in this case, Jahim picked a bear, so I was the papa bear, and he was the baby bear.

Anyway, to make a long story short, Jahim jumped into the catfish pond out by the garden, looking for fish and, of course, I had to go in behind him. And that's the end of our little dirty story."

"Oh, I understand," said Virgil, nodding her head. "Now you and Jahim better go get cleaned up before someone sees you and you know who I'm talking about."

As soon as Jahim and Steve left, Virgil and Liza burst into laughter. Jahim and Steve peeked into the living room, Liza and Virgil immediately stopped laughing. When they left, they continued to laugh again.

"I knew that they were going to laugh at us. They always did it at home," said Jahim.

"Don't worry, we'll pay them back. But first, we have to get out of these muddy clothes, send them down the laundry chute, and as soon as we get cleaned up, we will pay Aunt Liza and Mommy Virgil a little visit, before Rose come up here and visit us for making such a mess."

Steve took a big black bag off the shelf inside of his closet and pulled out several water guns. "Which one do you want?"

"I want that one," Jahim, pointed at a big orange one.

"You would pick the bigger one. All right, you have the double-barrel with two tanks and I have the plain old machine gun. Are you sure that you don't want to trade?"

Jahim shook his head in disagreement.

"Okay, I guess I'll just have to settle with this one."

"What kind of guns are these?" asked Jahim. "There are no bullets."

Steve laughed. "Okay, these are to be filled with water, not bullets. Let me show you how it's done. Come into the bathroom with me." Jahim followed Steve.

Steve and Jahim filled their weapons to the rim.

"Now let's go and tear those hair do's up." Shouted Steve!

"Ah right!" replied Jahim.

"That's the spirit, but we'll have to make a plan to get them outside. I don't want Rose to teach you any of her foreign language."

"I can do it," said Jahim. "Stay." Jahim motioned for Steve to stay where he was.

Jahim gave Steve his gun to hold while he went back into the living room with Liza and Virgil and sat in a chair by the window, without saying a word.

"Jahim, are you mad at us for laughing at you earlier?" asked Virgil.

"If you are mad at us, we're very sorry if we upset you," said Liza.

"I'm okay."

"If there is anything that we can do to make it up to you, just let us know," said Virgil.

"Sit with me outside," Jahim happily replied.

Liza and Virgil went outside with Jahim.

Jahim sat on the long cushioned bench for only a few minutes between Liza and Virgil before he jumped up and ran around the house. Liza and Virgil hardly noticed, since they were so deep off into their conversation again.

Steve was waiting for Jahim to meet him on the side of the house.

Steve gave Jahim back his water gun. "When I count to three, we'll run around to them and aim straight for their hair. Do you remember how to use that thing?"

"Yes," said Jahim.

"Okay, troops, one, two, three. Let's go," said Steve.

"Liza and Virgil saw Steve and Jahim coming towards them from behind the house, but it was too late to do anything. Jahim and Steve soaked their hair and clothing to the skin.

After chasing them around in circles a couple of more times, Virgil managed to open the door and she and Liza ran inside. Steve and Jahim shot at the patio door.

"Steven, now you quit teaching Jahim bad habits," screamed Virgil through a small opening in the door. Steve and Jahim stopped shooting.

"We were just having a little fun," laughed Steve.

"At our expense," said Liza.

"You had it at our expense earlier," said Steve.

"That's different," said Liza.

"How?" asked Steve.

Liza paused a moment. "I don't know, but it's not the same," said Liza. Steve and Jahim laughed as they walked away.

"Well, Liza, there's only one thing to do."

"What's that Virgil?"

"We have to go and get our hair done and buy a new outfit."

"Who's paying for all of this?"

"Don't worry about it, It's on Steve."

Virgil picked up Steve's wallet off the bar and waved it at him before she went upstairs to change clothes.

"You see, women are spoiled," Steve told Jahim. "They want to do bad things to you, but they don't want you to do bad things to them. They're getting ready right now to go and get their hair done and probably buy a new outfit, but they won't stop there. Oh no, they'll have to have the purse, the shoes, the whole works."

"Are they mad?" asked Jahim.

"No, they're probably glad."

"Why?" asked Jahim.

"Women are a strange group of species. Your Mommy Virgil was a little angry a little while ago. Some women will be mad at you one minute, but if you give them a credit card or even cash money, they're not mad anymore. They'll go and run up your credit card bill or spend all of your money and forget all about the ordeal for a while."

"What's a credit card?" asked Jahim.

"Can you remember the first night when Virgil and I took you shopping. Oh, I guess you weren't paying attention, but anyway a credit card is another kind of money. You can sometimes use it instead of using money," said Steve, trying not to make it too complicated.

"I think I understand, I can use one when I don't have pocket change, for my wallet," said Jahim.

Steve laughed. "You don't quite understand it yet, but I see that your English has improved one hundred percent."

"American women are . . . different than my people back in Africa. My teacher says that I should wait before I get hitched. These American women are strange and besides, I don't have any money to give them."

"Don't worry, big guy, you're a very smart kid and it won't be long before you'll want to learn the ways of the American women. Let me give you some advice, you'll learn quickly to whom you should stay away from and to whom you can't afford.

Just keep sticking around your aunt and Mommy. They can both teach you a lot without uttering a word."

Jahim laughed. "You're right about Mommy Virgil. She's the one I can't afford. I looked in her closet one day and she has more shoes than all the people back home in my village. Aunt Liza, I know she is the kind that I should stay away from.

She is . . . she is . . . I can't think of the word that best tells you about Aunt Liza," said Jahim.

"Sneaky," said Steve.

"That's a good one," said Jahim.

"About those shoes in your Mommy Virgil's closet, she doesn't even wear them all, and the word for that is waste, but I will say that sometimes she takes some of the old ones down to the flea market, sells them, and give the money to needy families, so some of it is going to a good cause.

I spoiled her, so now I'm paying the price."

"I can learn a lot in this family. All I have to do is pay attention."

"What did I tell you? You're too smart for your own good."

Jahim gave Steve a big smile.

"You know, Jahim, I never really spent my money on just me. How about you and I go and buy us some toys?"

"All right!" yelled Jahim as he ran to get into the limo.

"No limo today, Jahim. I only use that thing when I don't feel like driving. Besides, we don't need any pushy limo driver asking us how long are we going to be. Let's take my Jeep." Jahim jumped into the driver's seat.

"Oh no, not yet," said Steve.

"Later?" asked Jahim.

"Yes," said Steve. Jahim put his head down.

"Let me tell you a little secret. The reason why I won't let you drive is because I think that your grandfather wants to be the first one to teach you." Steve put one finger over his lips. "Don't tell him that I told you."

Jahim smiled. "I can keep it to myself."

"Good, now get over and buckle up," said Steve.

Chapter 11

Virgil came rushing into the restaurant.

"Hello, dear, I'm glad that you could join me." Steve, stood up and pushed Virgil with her chair under the table.

"Sorry I'm late, it's Charles's fault," said Virgil.

"How is it his fault?"

"Because after I left the hairdresser, I called Charles from my car, to tell him to come out in fifteen minutes to help me with my bags. I was in a hurry, but it took me a little longer than I expected. When I arrived, Charles had stepped back into the house for a couple of minutes. That's why I'm late."

Steve laughed. "Is that the best that you could come up with?"

"Well, I would've had a better one, but I didn't have enough time to think of it."

"Unfortunately, our guest didn't have time to hang around. They are very upset with you."

Virgil looked as if she didn't care.

"Well, don't look so upset," said Steve.

"I'm sorry, dear. It's just that I've never met these people. Therefore, I haven't any reason to be upset."

"I understand, that's why I invited them over for dessert and cocktails later on."

Virgil ignored Steve's last statement. "Steve, have you eaten?"

"No, just a salad."

"Well, could we eat somewhere else? I don't really feel like being high society today."

"I was hoping that you'd say that. Let's go get something greasy and fattening, like a large pizza, with everything on it." Steve got up from the table, leaving a twenty-dollar tip for him and his absent guests. After

125

Virgil's and Steve's pizza fest, they arrived home just minutes before their guest arrived.

Charles answered the door and announced. "Mr. William and his wife Ashe are here to see you."

Steve and Virgil followed Charles into the dining room where Mr. William and Ashe were waiting.

"It's a pleasure finally getting to meet you," Mr. Williams shook Virgil's hand.

"It's nice to meet you also, Mr. Williams."

"Please call me Will, everyone else does."

"Okay, Will it is," said Virgil.

"This is my wife, Ashe."

"I've heard so much about you, Virgil," said Ashe.

"Gosh, and I haven't heard one thing about you," said Virgil as she looked at the tall, slender lady with pretty long black hair and a great smile.

"Let me do the explaining, said Steve. Will is a director and producer. He wants to put the band in his new movie, called *Music Life*.

It's about the life and times of a famous musician, and he wants our band to perform at the beginning and at the end of the movie."

Virgil gave Steve a strange stare. "It's not about us, it's fiction," Steve added, reading Virgil's face.

Virgil placed her hand on her chest. 'What a relief,' she thought.

Just then, Charles came in with dessert. "Dessert is now served." Ashe took one look at the dessert tray.

"Fried ice cream!" she screamed. "I haven't had this in years and I'm not turning it down either. I'll just have to starve myself for a week." Ashe put a big spoonful in her mouth without waiting for the others.

"You'll have to excuse my wife. If she wouldn't starve herself so much, she wouldn't have to miss all the pleasures of good desserts as much."

"That's okay, let her go. She can afford to gain a few pounds," said Virgil.

"You could afford to put a few pounds on yourself," said Will.

"Oh no," said Virgil. "One hundred and twenty-five pounds is as far as I can go. It doesn't matter how much I eat, I can't gain a pound. This is how I plan to look twenty-five years from now." Everyone laughed.

"Not if you keep eating the way that you do," said Steve. Virgil rolled her eyes at him. "Oh come on, I was only kidding. You look great." Steve walked over and gave Virgil a big hug.

After dessert, Will got out of his chair.

"Steve", said Will if this is the right time, I'd like to see those videos and listen to that demo of yours."

"Oh yes." I was enjoying our conversation and almost forgot why you came here." Steve walked over to where Ashe and Virgil were talking.

"Honey, I'm going to go and show Will the tape and let him hear the new demo. Show Ashe the house or something, we will be back in say forty-five minutes." Steve gave Virgil a big kiss.

Ashe turned to face Virgil. "So I guess it's just you and me."

"Would you like to see the house? Let's start upstairs."

'Here I go again, giving another tour,' Virgil thought.

"Why not? Upstairs sounds fine." said Ashe.

Virgil led the way to the stairs case, Ashe followed.

Virgil stopped suddenly in front of April's room and Ashe bumped into her.

"Whoops! Excuse me."

"That's okay." 'What a clump,' Virgil thought.

Virgil continued the tour.

"This is my daughter's room. Her name is April. She's not here right now because my mother keeps stealing her from us. Every time that she doesn't sleep here with us, I have to go over there just to kiss her good-nite."

"You're lucky. Sometimes I think that my mom wants nothing to do with my kids and here you, are unable to keep your mom away from yours."

Virgil kept going, as she passed up several rooms before stopping in front of Jahim's room. "This is my little buddy Jahim's room." Ashe stepped into the room to get a better look.

"Who is Jahim?"

"It's a long story. Let's move on." Virgil closed the door.

Virgil turned on the light to the basement. "Watch your step."

"Gosh, this house is amazing."

"I know, especially this part down here. It's like a whole house by itself."

Ashe walked over to what seemed to be a playroom. "What's this? A nursery?"

"Something like that. It's for when our company brings kids to our gatherings. This is where they eat and have fun. It's also heavily secured with at least twelve helpers while the kids are inside, depending on the amount of children there are."

"It looks like a big playground and house all in one, I wouldn't mind being a kid down here while you do all the fake smiles upstairs."

"I know, isn't it irritating to smile at someone that you really don't want to smile at?"

"Yeah, let's not talk about it. It gives me the creeps," said Ashe. "Let's finish the tour, what's behind this door in the corner?"

Virgil went over and opened the door.

Ashe peeked inside.

"This creepy thing is the wine cellar. Do you want to go inside?"

"No way, there might be spiders in there."

"I know the feeling. The butlers get the wine from here, because no one can get the maids to come near this room."

"I don't blame them. I've seen enough of this room for the night, myself," said Ashe.

Virgil laughed. "We can end it here if you want."

"No, I want to go on. Let's look in this room with the black door," said Ashe.

"You don't want to go in there," said Virgil.

"Ah, come on."

"It's locked and I don't have the key."

"Girl, are you trying to hide something from me?"

Virgil thought for a minute. "Oh alright, but just for a minute." Virgil opened the door slowly and turned on the lights. Ashe's eyes widened as she looked around at all the shelves and shelves of sex toys.

Shit!" exclaimed Ashe. "Do you think that you have enough kinks?"

"Maybe," Virgil replied.

"Look at this one, it has one on both ends. Can I borrow some of your pride and jo—"

"No!" said Virgil, cutting her off before she could complete her sentence.

"Okay, fine," said Ashe. With that, Virgil turned off the lights and locked the door.

As Ashe walked out into the hallway, her mind was in a race of wondering questions.

"Do you guys use them often?" She found enough courage to ask.

"Sometimes," Virgil responded. "Are you ready to go back upstairs?" Virgil added.

Ashe waited until Virgil's back was turned, then she slipped the two-headed dick half-hidden in a flower pot on a table in the corner of the hallway.

"Wait!" exclaimed Ashe. "We didn't look behind the red door yet."

'She is so nosey.' Virgil was thinking to herself. "It's only a room," she replied.

Ashe begged. "Can I see it please?"

Virgil took the key out of her pocket and opened the door. This time, Ashe pushed the door open and turned on the lights. Ashe's eyes almost popped out of her head. "I can see why you didn't want me in this room. Look at all of this stuff!"

There is a dick-shaped bed, dick-shaped phone, lamps, and not to mention, the pussy-lip-shaped chair for two, and pussy and dick symbols on the curtains, sheets, and comforter, etc," exclaimed Ashe.

Ashe started walking around the room, poking and pinching on everything as if they were rolls of toilet paper. Virgil could even see her nipples trying to peek out from outside her blouse.

"I bet that you and Steve spend a lot of time in this room."

"Oh, not really," said Virgil. "Only on anniversaries and special occasions."

Ashe walked over to the bed to examine it. "How do you turn this thing on?"

There were several switches on the front panel of the head board, for four different movements. Round and round, up and down, back and forth, and fast or faster. Virgil flipped the switch to turn on the bed to show Ashe how it worked.

Ashe fell backwards on the bed and began to move around and around on her back with the movement of the bed exposing to Virgil that she clearly didn't have on any underwear under her stockings, as she whirled her ass around on the bed in her short skirt.

"You're having way too much fun on that bed all by yourself," Virgil said.

"Well, I'd have more fun if I had company."

Virgil turned off the bed. Ashe stood up and adjusted her vest and short skirt. "Sorry."

"No problem," said Virgil.

Ashe looked, over in the direction of the closet. "What's in there?"

Virgil walked over to the closet and opened the door. "Does this answer your question?" Virgil stood back so that Ashe could get a better view of the whole closet.

Ashe stepped in and immediately picked up a long, dark, reddish-tanned dildo off the shelf.

"This thing is huge, how long is it?" she said.

"Thirty inches," replied Virgil.

"Thirty inches!" Ashe repeated. "The head of this is as big as four of my fingers." Next Ashe went through a series of strange events. She walked over to the pussy-lip chair and pretended to stick the dildo in the big opening in front of the chair.

She rubbed the gigantic toy up and down her inner thighs, rode it like a horse, threw it on the bed and jumped on top of it, she moved her clit wildly all over it, and Virgil took one look at her and shook her head in disgust.

"Do you mind?"

Ashe was so busy that she didn't realize that Virgil was talking to her. Virgil repeated herself this time, she said it louder.

"Do you mind?"

Ashe jumped up and, without responding, returned the big toy back in its original place. Virgil noticed that Ashe turned her attention towards the book collection. Virgil rolled her eyes into the back of her head.

'Why not? But I get to pick the book,' Virgil thought. Virgil went over and picked up her favorite book. "Males and Drag Queens." She opened it and picked out a short story. They both sat down and took turns reading.

After they finished the book, Virgil removed herself from the bed.

"Damn! said Virgil. I'm going to have to fuck my husband the minute that you and Will leave."

Ashe stood up. "Why do you have to wait, when you can fuck me right now?"

Virgil took one step away from Ashe. "Sorry, but I need something that is going to stick to my stomach."

Suddenly Ashe ran out of the room and returned with the two-headed dildo that she had stashed in the hallway.

"Will this help?" Virgil took another step back and Ashe took two steps up.

"It's not the same," said Virgil.

Ashe used one end of the two heads to raise up Virgil's loose-fitting skirt. "Don't knock it, unless you tried it," and with that, she proceeded to slide the same end of the dildo in between Virgil's upper thighs.

She moved so close to Virgil that she could feel Ashe's breath on the side of her face, making the lump in between her upper thighs tingle her with delight.

"I think that we'd better see what our husbands are up to," said Virgil breaking away from Ashe's spell and straightening her skirt.

"No," whispered Ashe. "I've got to have you."

"No, you don't. Save that energy for your husband."

"I would if he knew how to take care of my needs. He can only last ten minutes or less, and I never get to come. We only do it one way, and he thinks that hopping up and down on top of me is love-making. I'm so hungry for some good loving.

I jack off three to four times a week to keep from going out into the streets. But, sometimes I need another person to hold and talk to while, I'm getting my groove on.

I would appreciated it if you could just fuck me for a little while, with the dildo to help me out before I go home and get disappointed again." Ashe said with that puppy-dog look in her eyes, she took a long look at Virgil, and Virgil returned the look, feeling sorry for her.

Ashe suddenly grabbed Virgil's face, giving her one of her most famous French kisses. Their breasts smashed into each other like some kind of head-on collision as they wrapped their arms around each other tightly.

Ashe unzipped Virgil's skirt in the back and squeezed her tight ass through her panties. Since Virgil didn't have on panty hoses, that made it all the better.

Virgil, finally moved away from Ashe and let her skirt drop around her ankles, and she just stepped out of it and kicked it to the side.

They took turns removing each other's clothing until they both stood stalked naked. Ashe took Virgil's hand and lead her to the bathroom.

"This has to be perfect." She turned the water on in the shower, stepped inside, and held her hand out for Virgil to join her.

After watering Virgil down from head to toe and soaping down her whole body, she then took a razor off the side of the tub and began to shave Virgil's pubic hairs.

Afterward, Ashe took her turn, while Virgil shaved her. After the shaving party was all done, they both admired each other's work.

"So, how do you like it?" asked Ashe.

Virgil looked down at her bare shaved pussy. "It's great, I feel free and refreshed."

"Good!" exclaimed Ashe. "Don't dry off yet, I want to oil you down and slither and slide all over your body."

Virgil gave her a wicked laugh as she walked over to the bed and threw off the comforter, so that oil wouldn't get all over it. Ashe slowly walked over. "Lie down and let me rub some of this oil all over your nicely shaved cunt." Virgil obeyed.

Upon finishing her kinky quest, Ashe laid on top of Virgil to bare meows together as they rolled over and over on the bed, hugging, and kissing until

Ashe interrupted the steamy foreplay by getting their two-headed friend and formally introducing it to Virgil's waiting twat.

Ashe sat down and positioned herself in front of Virgil and she in turn took the other end of the two-headed mate and inserted it inside of her wet glove. As the two moved smoothly together, their bodies became closer and closer.

As their insides swallowed the dick whole. Ashe let out a huge scream when she made contact with Virgil's flowing twat.

"Fuck me!" Ashe said, Virgil picked up the pace, and Ashe met her every move.

"Ohh! This dick feels so good," said Virgil.

"Yes, it does," whispered Ashe.

Virgil and Ashe were so busy cuddling, kissing, and fucking, that they didn't realize that their husbands were in the T.V. room, watching their wives fuck the shit out of each other. "I didn't think that your wife would go for it," said Will.

"We do this kind of thing to each other all of the time."

"Look how big my wife's mouth gets when your wife's breast is in it," said Will. "I wish my wife was in here blowing me right now. My dick is so hard I think I'm going to come all over myself."

"Not yet, we all have to go in there together," said Steve.

"I bet those pussies are really wide right now. I just want to swim in Ashe's cum and maybe even drown."

Steve grabbed his groin and unbuttoned the top button to his pants. "Sounds good to me."

"Yea, I'm so horny that I could suck my own dick," said Will. Steve laughed.

"Patience, Will, patience."

"Oh look! They're taking it out. Damn, look how wet and silky that thing is. What is your wife doing? Oh my, and you can see it good too, Ashe's hole is big. Your wife has strapped on another dildo and is taking my place," cried Will.

Meanwhile, back with the girls . . .

Virgil changed her strap on again to please Ashe thoroughly. "Bend over onto the bed," said Virgil. Virgil then wet her big friend with her own juices and pushed her private friend until he disappeared into Ashe's pool hole.

"You've been a bad girl," Virgil jerked Ashe by the hair and spanked her soft ass, while pounding into her hole, causing Ashe to scream with a mixture of pain and pleasure.

"That's it. Fuck this pussy and wear it out," Ashe screamed.

Will grabbed his crouch and moved back and forth at the T.V. screen. "Save some for me! Save some for me! I can't take this anymore, Steve, can we go now?"

Steve in turn unzipped his pants. "Not yet," he said calmly.

"But when and how long do I have to wait?" Will cried.

Instead of answering Will, Steve stuck his hands inside of his underwear and begin to message his cock that was on the verge of ejaculating.

By this time, Ashe and Virgil had switched up, and Ashe was drilling deep off into Virgil's snatch, expressing water waves with her ass.

"Look at our wives. See the looks on their faces. They're enjoying every bit of what's going on. This makes me wonder what she need me for," said Will.

"She still needs you. Come on, let's go down there and crash that party." Steve got off the couch, with his weapon in hand and headed towards the basement.

Will didn't waste any time pushing Virgil aside and entering Ashe's slippery pussy with one big thrust. There was quite a lot of moaning in that room after Steve arrived and joined in, letting his dick slide in and out of Virgil's tunnel of love.

The smell of sex was thick in the air, along with the loud slapping noises of wet pussies. Will, on the other hand, was growing weak. He was having a hard time keeping his pace after waiting so long.

"I can't hold it anymore!" he yelled! As he flooded Ashe's snatch with a big flow of his cum, but he didn't let that stop him, as he continued to bounce up and down, keeping up with the rest of the party until Ashe screamed along with Virgil.

And in last place was Steve with the loudest roar, while Virgil rushed greedily to catch his hot spurts.

For about two hours, no one moved and no one said a word. Virgil was the first to break the silence.

"I'm going to the shower," she said in a low voice. Virgil slowly but surely made her way onto the floor. She took two steps before turning around to grab Ashe's arm to come with her.

While Ashe and Virgil were in the shower, Steve and Will cut off the light and joined them, with tools in hand again, picking up where they left off.

The party lasted for several hours until Will and Ashe decided that their wells were dry and they should go home. The two couples parted their ways at the front door and Steve and Virgil retired to their room. That's where they realized that all sex is not good sex. Their bodies were tired and it was hard just to drag themselves to the breakfast table the next morning.

"Gosh, I can't believe it's been a whole day and I can still feel a little pain from that dildo that Ashe and I shared."

Steve laughed as he pulled her close. "I think that it was my dildo that made your stomach hurt, and the way that you two were going at it, you should have some kind of pain."

Virgil thought for a second. "But it was good and worth it."

"Which one felt the best to you? That fake dildo or" (Steve put Virgil's hand inside of his pants) "my dildo?"

"Well, you know the answer to that."

"I know it. Yes, but I want to hear it from you."

"Yours, sweetheart," said Virgil, then she gave Steve a long hard kiss, followed by a tight hug.

"Did you put Ashe up to flirting with me?"

"Yes, of course. Will and I were watching from the Studio. I was hoping that you would get carried away and let yourself go. I'm just glad that you and I are able to do these things together.

I mean, there're not too many men that would team up with his buddy, to clean out his wife's ears with cum."

Virgil gave Steve another kiss. "You are the best."

Steve was the first to pull away. "Alright, Virgil. Let's not put ourselves in the hospital."

"Don't worry, I won't hurt myself. I need my energy for April and Jahim, when we take them to the park today."

"That's right," said Steve. "I will go and pick up April. When you're finished picking in your food, you can go outside and tell Jahim the good news."

"Where outside is he?"

"He's at the pool house, entertaining Pedro with his not—so—magic tricks." Virgil almost choked on her toast with laughter, and Steve had to pat her back.

"Are you okay?"

"I'm fine. We'll be ready when you come back."

After Steve left, Virgil repeated what Steve said about Jahim and laughed again. She sat alone and finished her breakfast before heading towards the pool house without shoes or socks.

"Jahim," she called.

"I'm here in the pool house." he hollered back.

Before answering Jahim, Virgil waited until she got to the doorway of the Pool House.

"What are you doing here?"

"I was showing Pedro some of my magic tricks, and he was showing me how to use the computer," said Jahim, obviously excited!

Virgil smiled at Jahim and said. "You go and get washed up, and I'll be there in a minute."

"Okay, Mommy Virgil."

Virgil watched as Jahim disappeared around the corner of the house, Virgil turned to Pedro. "The next time that you want to show Jahim something, I'd appreciate it if you would get permission first."

"No problem," said Pedro.

Virgil gave Pedro a mean look, rolled her eyes at him and walked away and, halfway to the corner of the house where she last saw Jahim, she turned and gave him another bad look.

She entered the house and found Jahim in his room.

"Are we going somewhere?" asked Jahim. "Rose said that I have to take a shower and put on some more clothes, but I'm not dirty. I took a shower yesterday. Why do I have to take another shower when I'm not even dirty?"

"I tell you what, young man. If you don't take a shower, then you won't go to the park with us."

Jahim jumped up and down. "Yes! Yes! Can I wear my new baseball cap?"

"Why, sure you can." Jahim skipped happily around the room a couple of times before settling down to take a shower. Steve returned with April in less than an hour. They were loaded in the car and ready to go to the park.

Chapter 12

"I take it that you didn't have any trouble with Mother over April?" said Virgil.

"No, not this time. Only because she and her Witch Hazel friends are going to play bingo," said Steve with a big outburst of laughter.

Virgil also laughed at Steve's joke. "That wasn't a nice thing to say about my mother's friends. She probably will go and have a drink tonight. That is the only reason that she let you have the baby." Virgil paused and said, "Bad Mom."

"Come on, Virgil, your mother is allowed to drink if she wants to."

Virgil thought about that for a couple of seconds. "Well, anyway, I'll leave that alone. Don't use those kinds of words in front of Jahim. We don't want any of these conversation to get back to my mother."

"Whoops!" said Steve. "He's not paying any attention to us anyway. He's too busy playing with April."

Before Steve pulled out of the driveway, he sorted out the CD that he wanted to hear on their trip to the park.

"We should take the Jeep more when we go on trips like this one," said Virgil.

"That was the plan until I came outside this morning and found Liza's big Bronco parked behind it, but she's nowhere to be found. All of these parking spaces, and she thought that putting her Jolly Green Giant behind my Jeep was the best place to be.

She was parked so awkward that I couldn't even squeeze through without tearing up her truck or mine," said Steve, getting very irritated the more he talked about it. "If I would've gotten one scratch on it, she would've received a fat bill from me."

Virgil turned in the direction of Steve. "I know, sweetheart, I know."

Steve realized that Virgil wasn't taking him seriously, and he chuckled to himself. "I'm going to have to get rid of you."

"You can't get rid of me," Virgil immediately replied.

"Why not?"

"Because we have too much dirt on each other. Besides what other man or woman are we going to find to do what we do together?"

"Okay, you got me, but I still don't want my jeep scratched."

"Steve, I wish that you wouldn't praise this vehicle so much."

"You're right, but it's hard. I'll try, I could improve a lot faster if I had a little therapy from my wife later on." Steve grabbed Virgil's waist.

"Steve!" Yelled Virgil. "Have you forgotten about the kids?"

"Of course not, baby. They're the reason why we're going to the park in the first place. If you didn't get so excited when I touch you, it would seem natural." Steve gave her one of his most sexual eye contacts.

"Cut that out," Virgil said in a whisper. "I don't know about Mr. Jahim. He talks and thinks like he's been in this life before. He catches on way too fast for his age. I bet if we put him into high school right now, they'd probably suggest college."

"I know just what you are talking about on that one," Steve butted in. "Two weeks ago, he and I went to the store and when we were at the check-out counter, Jahim pulled out that little calculator remote control car that I bought him. He had everything, including tax, added up before the cashier was even done with the scanning.

"The cashier suggested that he could have her job or send him to a special school for advanced students."

"A special school! Virgil repeated, with excitement."

"Now, now, don't get too excited. We'll have to get Jahim's say so on this one. He's still a kid at heart. I tell you what, we can bring it up at the next family meeting, then we'll hear what he has to say."

Steve found the park to be extremely crowded. He drove around and around the parking lot of the park, trying to find a spot wide enough so that when he parked, there would be enough room on each side so that his vehicle wouldn't get dented.

After riding around again with no luck with his investigation of the parking lot.

Steve let out a big sigh. "I think I'm going to let you and Jahim out in the front, I'll find a parking space, then April and I will catch up with you two in a few minutes.

Jahim was so excited that he got out of the jeep without even looking down to see where he was stepping and almost tripped in a muddy hole in the grass. "Wow!" exclaimed Jahim. "I—"

Jahim's words were cut off as a little girl passed him with a big, tall pink—and—blue cotton—looking object on a stick. Pulling on Virgil's shirt, he cried, "What's that thing that she is eating?"

Virgil laughed, then replied, "That is called cotton candy."

"Cotton candy?"

"Yes, it's a smooth kind of sweet cotton that melts in your mouth on contact."

"That's amazing, can I try some?" Jahim jumped up and down.

"You sure can. You will try and experience a lot of things today, so keep the quantities to a minimum. Remember, it's your day and you don't want to make yourself sick by trying too much of everything."

As soon as Jahim was running his thoughts of excitement through his mind, Steve and April arrive.

"Did you guys find a parking spot in this state?" Virgil asked.

"Of course not, we had to park in another one."

"Now what's on the agenda for today?" Steve said as he turned to Jahim.

"Cotton candy!" screamed Jahim as he jumped up and down!

Steve walked closer to Jahim and bent down to talk to him face-to-face. "Now what do you know about cotton candy?"

Jahim stepped one step closer to Steve. "I know enough to know that I want some of it," explained Jahim as he rubbed his nose against Steve's.

"We'll, since you put it to me like that, let's go and get some cotton candy. I'll even race you there."

Virgil and April watched as the two boys raced off.

Virgil and her family spent the whole entire day in the park. Jahim rode all the rides, tasted a bit of everything, and April fed the animals.

On the way home, Virgil looked into the back seat. "Now doesn't that look familiar?" she said. "I know that Jahim acts like a grown-up, but now he looks like you, laid out in the back seat after a long gig."

"Right now, I think that he and April are dreaming about the same dream," said Steve.

"You know, Steve, I really hope that these pictures come out okay. I want Jahim's family to know that he's doing okay and that they don't have to worry about him.

I'll send these pictures along with the clothes that I'll send to his mother, grandmother, and the toys to his younger siblings."

Steve turned and faced Virgil at the next stop light.

"What?" she said with a puzzled look. "I didn't pay that much for them."

"That's not why I'm looking at you, Virgil. I'm looking at you because I love you."

"I love you too, Daddy," said Virgil with a smile as she leaned over and gave him a big kiss on the cheek.

"About those things that you're going to send to Jahim's family, don't forget to send them to the secret address or someone else will be wearing and playing with the things that you bought."

"You're right about that one," Virgil said. "I just hope that the colors that I'll send are okay. I'll even send sandals."

Steve rested his hand on Virgil's leg. "I know that you want to spoil them, but try not to send anything too fancy. We wouldn't want to make waves between them and the other people in the village.

They have enough problems already. Now, is there anything else that you're sending over there that I don't know about?" said Steve as he gave Virgil a love tap on the cheek.

Are you talking to me?" said Virgil, pointing to herself.

"Yes you, Virgil. I've been married to you long enough to know you. Now what else are you sending that I have no knowledge of?"

"Well."

"Come on, spit it out, girl."

"Okay, okay. I spoke with *Kwame*, and he stated that it would be okay to send the sugar-free candy, that I'm going to send. He said that he'll explain to them that it's not food and it is not made to eat all at once."

"I knew it!" Steve shouted. "I knew it!" Steve turned to Virgil. "Don't I know my wife, huh?"

Virgil didn't answer.

In a bolded voice, Steve said, "Answer me, woman."

Virgil just laughed to herself, but still didn't answer.

Later on that night, when Virgil and Steve were lying outside under the stars . . .

"Honey, what would you think or do if you came home one day and found Jahim's whole family, including his cousins and maybe some friends, sitting in our living room?"

In a very low voice, Steve said. "Could you just save one person at a time please? Let's wait until we adjust to Jahim first, before we send for the rest of Africa?"

"Okay, sweetie. I'm just so excited to help someone in need, which are those who are less fortunate than we are."

Steve let out a big laugh. "I just think that you're excited to help exercise your right to shop with my credit cards."

"Well, that's true too. A girl has to do what a girl has to do."

Chapter 13

"I got it! I got it!" yelled Steve as he came running out into the garden, where Virgil and Rose were planting flowers.

"What did you get?" asked Virgil.

"I got the gig!"

"Which one?" asked Rose.

"The big one in San Francisco," Steve managed to squeeze out, all in one breath.

"That's great, honey! When exactly do you leave?"

"One week from today. Jahim, his tutor, and I will leave tomorrow night. You and April can leave sometime between Friday and Saturday."

"Sounds good to me," said Virgil.

Steve almost turned to go back to the house, but stopped. "There's one more thing. Rose, you always said that you've never been to any of my concerts. Well, here's your chance.

Virgil could use some help. It's kind of hard to carry a baby and all of those shopping bags."

Virgil gave Steve a small pinch on the arm. "Watch it, Steve," Virgil laughed.

"So what do you say?" Steve held his arms out to Rose and gave her his best hug.

"I say yes, yes, and yes!" said Rose, returning Steve's hug.

"Good, because I already told the other maids that you'll be out of town. They'll be able to manage without you, since there'll be no one in the household to cleanup after. Jahim he'll be with me the whole time at rehearsals.

I'll give him cymbals and some shakers, and he'll be with me on stage. I know he'll get a real kick out of that."

Pedro waited until Jahim and Steve left before he paid Virgil a little visit. He slithered in through an open patio door that Charles left unlocked, while he was taking a swim.

Pedro looked carefully over his shoulders, then quietly took the stairs to Virgil's room. Once inside, he noticed right away that Virgil must be taking a bath, because of the sweet smell of aroma and soft music coming from her bathroom.

He peeked into the bathroom to find her emerged in a steamy tub of bubbles, with black patches over her eyes and a damp towel rested on her forehead.

'She looks so peaceful,' he thought. He wanted her badly, but now wasn't the time. He waited patiently on the outside of her balcony curtains, watching as she finally came out of the bathroom, naked and dripping wet.

Her body glistened from the bath oil, and her nipples were hard from the breeze of the open balcony window. She grabbed a big bath towel off the bed and walked out onto the balcony.

Pedro disappeared out of view, as she spread the towel on a sofa chair and laid on it to dry off in the cool breeze. Pedro's pants poked out somewhat strangely in the front as he watched Virgil's body.

Before long, the breeze was beginning to feel too intense, so Virgil decided she'd better come in and put on something before she catch a cold and was too sick to travel.

Pedro had a hard time maintaining himself as Virgil bent over and looked in her bottom dresser drawer to find some nightwear.

When Virgil went into the bathroom to brush her teeth, Pedro thought that this would be the perfect opportunity to come out of his little hiding place, remove his shorts and straddle behind Virgil's ass as she leaned over the sink area.

Virgil raised her head up quickly as she felt the hard lump behind her and the face of Pedro in the mirror. "I wish that you wouldn't sneak up behind me that way."

"You know that you don't want me to stop doing it," said Pedro in his most sexy voice.

"Yes, I do," Virgil said in loud whisper as she tried to loosen Pedro's firm grip. But, every time that Virgil would loosen the grip, Pedro would jerk his hand back into place.

"If you don't want it, just say so, and I'll leave."

Virgil looked into the mirror and she met Pedro's gaze. "I don't want it."

Pedro let Virgil go free and pulled up his shorts. "So just leave the same way that you came in." Virgil rested her finger on the light switch in the bathroom. "After you," she barked.

Pedro pretended to turn and leave, but made an about-face instead and bent Virgil over the sink. He had such a firm hold over her that she couldn't even move. He then pulled down his shorts first before he snatched off her underwear.

He drove his hardened dick deeper and deeper, and Virgil's pussy lips swallowed him right up. She spread her legs wide while Pedro's thighs banged hard against her plumped juicy ass. "I knew that you wanted me to fuck you. You can't get enough of this good dick, can you?"

Virgil didn't answer.

"That's okay. You don't have to answer because I'm going to wear this pussy out for making me wait so long." Pedro then picked Virgil up with his dick still inside of her. Positioned her on the bed with her face on the pillow and her ass in the air and continued to drill her hole with his power drill.

Virgil was moving every way possible, including gripping the sheets and screaming his name. For what seemed like an hour Pedro punished and tingled Virgil's whole body.

Pedro had a huge eruption and Virgil could feel his load shoot into her as he gripped her hips for support.

A few minutes passed and Pedro started to regain some strength back, so he let his dick flop out of Virgil's drenched pussy and told her to turn over. "Suck me," he ordered.

Virgil began to suck her cream off his cock right down to the balls. When they dropped out she'd put them both back into her mouth.

Pedro was fascinated by the way Virgil slurped his cock, he never took an eye off of her lips the whole time that she was doing him.

Soon, Pedro's cock became hard again and he was ready to do a repeat on Virgil. He wasn't the only one feeling the heat in that room. Virgil began to finger her erect pearl tongue, since it was full and firm again.

Virgil removed his hot rod from her mouth.

"So why don't you give me a round of bases? she asked.

"I think that I've given you enough innings. You're getting too spoiled for me," said Pedro.

Virgil went over and locked the bedroom door, then threw the key out of the balcony door. "I'm not going to put up with this anymore," she said. "You're going to give me the dick and you're going to fuck me and like it."

Pedro went over to the door to make sure that it was really locked. Virgil walked over to where Pedro was standing and reached for him, but he quickly moved out of the way of her reach.

"I don't have time to play games with you, Pedro," said Virgil with her hands placed on her hips now. Suddenly, Pedro grabbed Virgil and tried to tie her up with a nearby scarf on the bed, but Virgil turned quickly and grabbed his waist, pulling him close to her and wouldn't let go.

Pedro tried to undo her grip without causing her any real pain, but she wouldn't loosen the hold that she had on him.

They ended up falling onto the bed, wrestling and scuffing until Pedro fell off the bed and ended up in a secure tight spot in a corner between the bed and the chester drawer.

Virgil didn't hesitate to pounce on top of him and bucked him like he had done her earlier. He didn't like the fact that Virgil had gotten the best of him. He managed to wiggle his way out of his sticky situation, knocking Virgil off of him and reversing the role.

"Now who's in control?" Pedro snarled, while holding a firm grip on Virgil's plump breast and trying to feel every spot of her insides. Virgil rose to the occasion until they both weakened and a stream of thick and juicy cum leaked down Virgil's asshole.

Pedro stood up and moved his semi-hard dick up and down using his mind.

"Do you see that? That's called dick control when you can move your manhood up and down without using your hands." Virgil reached for Pedro again. "You can't have any more," he said.

"If I wanted some more, I'll just take it," she said, as she headed for the shower.

Pedro slipped into his shorts and tried the door again without thinking.

Virgil realized at the same moment that, the door was still locked and came out of the bathroom.

Seeing Pedro standing by the door, looking helpless made her laugh.

"Can I get out, please," said Pedro calmly.

"Don't you remember?" said Virgil as she continued to laugh. "I threw the key over the balcony."

"I know that! Don't you have another key?" said Pedro.

"I do, but it's not in this room. You'll just have to get on the phone and call Charles up here to get you out."

"Are you crazy? I can't let Charles see me up here in your bedroom with the door locked. I don't think that he even like me all that much. There's got to be another way."

Virgil pointed to the balcony. "Sure there is."

Pedro walked slowly towards the balcony and looked down, then at Virgil, and then down, and then towards Virgil again. Pedro shook his head as he looked down once more at how far it was to the ground.

"Now that's a thought, that I will think of no longer. I may be desperate, but not that desperate enough to break something."

"So what are you going to do?" "You can't stay in my room all night."

Pedro looked at Virgil. "Well, I'm not the one who threw the key over the balcony."

Virgil turned her head to laugh a little and back again to face Pedro. There was silence in the room for a moment. Finally, Virgil couldn't take it anymore and broke the silence.

"There is a key by the lamp over there on the far side of the room," Virgil said as she pointed in the direction of the key.

Pedro hesitated for a moment, hoping that this wasn't another one of her tricks, then he made a sudden move for the key, as if Virgil was going to race him to it.

After getting the key and opening the door, Pedro put one foot between the door and the other in the hallway. "I'll seek my revenge later." Virgil didn't respond as she closed the door behind him.

She waited until she knew that he was clear out of site. "I'll be waiting," she whispered to herself.

Chapter 14

The trip to San Francisco was enjoyable.

Virgil, Rose, and April had one hell of a view from behind stage . . .

"Oh my goodness!" said Rose, peeking out through the curtains. "There's no way that I would be able to perform in front of all of those people. I would probably faint and land flat onto my face."

Virgil walked over to the curtains. "Sssh!" she said pointing to Jahim, whom was being dressed by Steve on the other side of the room. "Jahim might hear us. We don't want to make him nervous. I think that Steve has probably done a good job at preparing Jahim for his first gig, but you'll never know what might happen when all of those people are staring you in the face."

"You're right," said Rose. "I won't speak of it again."

Minutes later, Steve and his crew went on stage for about two hours. The concert was a success and Jahim stole the show.

Of course Jahim was not going anywhere until he had a tour of the city before, going back to the hotel. Everyone was exhausted but Virgil. That night she just laid awake counting balloons, twiddling her thumbs, and tossing and turning while Steve laid fast asleep.

After a while, she couldn't take it anymore, so she slipped out of bed and tiptoed into the bathroom, grabbed her long, flowered colored satin robe, a small cup, and made her way out into the quiet halls of the huge hotel.

She was only four rooms down, when she heard a noise around the next corner. Virgil carefully walked towards the noise, peeked around the corner and realized it was only the night crew checking the ice machine.

Staying out of sight, Virgil waited until they were finished before she went over and begin filling her small cup with some of the bite-size ice cubes.

When her cup was full, she turned around just at the right time to bump right into one of the men that was there checking the icebox.

"Sorry, madam, I didn't mean to startle you," said the guy.

"That's okay," Virgil said shyly, as she studied the handsome piece like a trophy. "I should pay more attention to where I'm going."

"The reason that I returned is because I saw you peeking at us from behind that wall over there and I just want to give you some descent advice."

"Oh!" said Virgil, putting her hand on her hips, while she looked him dead into his eyes. "What kind of advice do you want to give me?"

"Well, to be honest, with you, Miss—"

"Virgil. The name is Virgil," she butted in.

"Well, okay, Virgil. As I was about to say, it isn't safe for a lady to walk alone at this time of the night by herself."

"You're right, Tyrone," said Virgil, taking a quick glance at his name tag. Virgil and Tyrone's eyes met, and after a few seconds, Virgil snapped out of it. "Maybe I should be getting back to my room" she said, breaking the silence.

"That's a good idea, and I'll be a gentleman and walk with you."

"You know, while you're escorting me back to my room, there is a place on the fifth floor, that I'll really like to see. I'd like to take a short look, before I retire for the rest of the night."

"Okay, but let's hurry. I'm supposed to be patrolling the halls, not giving sightseeing tours."

Stepping out of the elevator, Virgil eyes gazed as she looked around for the artwork that was pictured in the magazine. "There it is," she yelled and pointed to the sculpture near the back wall of the room.

"Shh," said Tyrone as he put his big hand gently over her lips. "You're going to wake someone."

Virgil ignored Tyrone as she walked over to the huge, life-size mechanical sculpture of a man slowing making love to a woman in the heat of the day on a big bed of beautiful flowers on a three-foot tall hill.

A small, slender lady with only a short sheer dress on is kneeling down near their heads and is wiping the sweat from his brows, while two big strong men without clothing, stand on each side of the couple and are fanning them with large palm fans.

Virgil couldn't believe what she was seeing. 'What a beautiful scene,' she thought to herself.

"So what do you see when you look at these sculptures?" Tyrone asked, as he walked up behind Virgil.

"I think that it's romantic. I don't think that I could have knowingly continued to carry on making love, if I knew that someone was drawing me and taking my pictures. That was my first initial thought when I first read about these sculptures. You can never tell. Maybe they didn't know or didn't care that someone was filming them." Tyrone took another look and said, "I think it's breathtaking, especially the way that the sweat is perspiring all over their bodies and the looks on their faces. The artist is very talented."

They both took one more look in a long silence. Tyrone slowly shook his head. "I know that the sex was good for them by those looks," he whispered. "I wonder why the artist made them appear in that way."

Virgil snapped out of her trance. "I'd better get back," she manages to say.

"Good idea," said Tyrone.

A funny thing happened as Virgil turned and walked towards the elevator. She tripped over her own two feet, and Tyrone ran to rescue her fall.

And as he was helping her recover her balance, he noticed that her robe had gaped open during the fall. He could see a ring-size view of her medium round breasts.

He was aroused immediately at that point. Virgil picked up on the sudden tightness in the front of his uniform pants.

Once inside the elevator, Virgil saw Tyrone staring at her boobs. Looking down at the opening in her robe, she untied and loosened the knot, letting her robe drop free to the floor. "You can suck them if you want."

Tyrone looked at Virgil, he wanted to suck them, but his feet were glued to the floor. After what seemed like minutes, Tyrone dragged his feet over to Virgil and began kissing her cleavage, and kicking the robe out of the way with his feet.

Virgil did what she could to control the vibes as Tyrone took turns running his tongue around each one of her nipples.

Suddenly, Tyrone forcefully pushed her against the elevator wall and was grinding her for two minutes nonstop until his strong body shivered. He released his grip and stepped back quickly.

"I'm so sorry, Virgil. I don't know what came over me. I hope that you will forgive me."

Virgil struggled to catch her breath, she managed to form a silly grin. "That's quite alright. I think that you should change those pants before someone sees them."

Tyrone looked down at his pants. "Maybe you're right. That spot maybe hard to explain, especially when it dries." The elevator stopped. Tyrone turned to get out. "Thank you." He waved good-bye and disappeared.

"It was different," said Virgil as the elevator closed.

'Four, three, two,' Virgil counted in her head, as the elevator headed in the direction of her floor. The door opened, and Virgil was about to get out, when she had to step aside for a couple and two maids with big carts.

That's when she found herself pushed to the back of the elevator and couldn't get out in time. The maids and their carts got out on the seventh floor, and the couple immediately pushed the button to the roof, without even asking Virgil where she wanted to go.

Virgil couldn't believe what was going on.

"Excuse me, where are we going?" asked Virgil, as if she didn't know.

"We're going to the roof, aren't we, Harry?" The woman said seductively, as she grabbed Harry's arm.

Harry put one hand underneath the woman's blouse. "Yes, we are, baby."

"Oh, Harry! You better stop that."

"Stop what?" said Harry in a fake surprise, this time grabbing one of her butt cheeks and laying on one slopping kiss that covered her whole mouth.

'Yuck!' Virgil thought to herself. 'I hate those kind.'

The couple didn't see the look on Virgil's face as she frowned. They were kissing so deeply and pressed so close that you'd need a crow bar to get them apart.

Virgil tried her best not to stare, but the woman's moans were getting louder as they took turns cramming each other around and around the elevator wall.

Suddenly Harry pushed the woman away and started banging on the elevator button until it jammed on the top floor. He then demanded that the woman kneel on the floor in front of him. She obeyed eagerly.

Harry unzipped his pants, letting them drop just before his knees and whipped out a small but very firm piece of meat, that stood about two inches long and two inches away from the woman's mouth.

For at least a minute, the woman just looked at the hard tool, without moving a muscle, and Harry looked over Virgil's body. Suddenly, Harry took a long, deep breath and spoke to the woman in a deep harsh tone, "Suck it!"

The woman immediately began to suck and blow him until he was almost at the point of no return. He then commanded her to stop, and in a language that Virgil couldn't understand, he must have told the woman to attack.

Because at that moment, the woman came over to Virgil and slapped her, and Virgil slapped her back. The woman grabbed Virgil, threw her face down on the floor of the elevator, she sat on her back, and tried to pulled off her satin underwear.

Virgil tried to throw her off, but this trick didn't work. It just made the woman hotter. She then pulled Virgil's panties halfway down and started to hump her ass.

This time, Virgil successfully threw the woman off her back. They struggled Virgil ended up on top of her she hit her hard across the head with her fist to pay her back, for making her face kiss the floor. This was when the woman locked both ankles tightly around Virgil's ankles and stretched them apart, ripping off her underwear in the process.

Virgil found herself in an unpredictable position as the woman rammed three fingers up Virgil's slippery cunt and started moving fast-forward, as if to accomplish a serious task.

'If I didn't know any better, I could bet you that these two had done this kind of thing before,' Virgil thought to herself, as she watched Harry come out of his statue state and released his steamy cum all over the back of the woman's neck and back.

"Get up!" said Harry to the woman. She quickly got up and they both fixed their clothes. Harry pulled a key out of his pocket, reset the elevator door, and they exit silently, the same way that they came in.

After they left, Virgil started at the wall in a confused daze. 'What in the hell?' She thought. Virgil then got off the elevator and took the stairs to her room, to avoid anymore incidents.

She made it inside of her room safely, cleaned herself up a bit then placed herself behind Steve and went into a deep sleep, dreaming of the ride home the next day.

Virgil and her family rode in a limo to the airport for a short ride home.

On the plane, Virgil was very quiet.

"What's the matter, my sweet pea?"

"Nothing, smooches, I'm fine." Virgil managed to say.

"If there's something bothering you, you can talk to me, and you already know that."

Virgil turned to face Steve. "Steve, I think we should lay off the adventures for a while because after what I told you this morning about last night, I just want to lay low for a little while."

I don't want you to be upset with me, but both situations were a little frightening and very strange."

"Let me make sure that I've got this correct, said Steve. You don't want to stop, you just want to take a pause then push play again later."

Virgil nodded her head slowly. "That's correct."

Steve put his arms around Virgil. They gave each other their most tightest squeeze. "I can never be mad at you, and I'll do anything for you. Anything." he added.

After Virgil and Steve arrived home, they waited a while before they got back into the freaky part of their lives. This time, someone had to be present at each sexual encounter to avoid any more elevator experiences like the last one.

The End.

This book is based on fictional characters. Although no means of safe sex was used in this book, doesn't mean that you shouldn't practice it.

There are several diseases that you can catch if you don't practice safe sex. They are listed off the internet as follows:

STD: or (Sexually Transmitted Diseases). is a bacterial or virtual infection that can be passed from person to person during sexual contact.

* Do you know that you could have an STD and not know it?
* Do you know that, in the United States, teens are at higher risk for getting an STD?
* Do you know that you can catch an STD without "Going all the way?"
* Do you know that women are more at risk than men for catching some STD?

There are more than twenty known diseases that can be transmitted sexually.

Fact or Fiction:

1. I'm not likely to get an STD the first time I have sex?

    On one hand, the majority of teens don't have STDs, so the odds are in your favor that you will have sex with someone who is not infected. On the other hand, there is no guarantee and no way to say to tell if you'll be safe. Many teens have contracted an STD during their first sexual encounter.

2. If I'm healthy, I can't catch STDs.

    False:. Although a strong immune system seems to protect you from disease, even healthy people can catch STDs.

3. If I wash thoroughly with soap and water immediately after sex, I won't I won't catch an STD.

    False:. Washing thoroughly with soap and hot water only slightly reduces the risk of catching an STD.

4. I'll know if I have an STD.

    False: Many STDs have no symptoms, particularly in women.

5. If I get an STD, I'll just take some penicillin and get rid of it.

    True/ and False: The treatment depends on the type of STD you have. Some STDs respond well to antibiotics,; others are incurable.

What is Chlamydia?

Chlamydia (pronounced Clud-mid-ee-ah), is caused by a tiny bacteria, Chlamydia Ttrachomat is (C. trachomatis). It can infect the urinary-genital area, the anal area, and sometimes the eyes, throat, and lungs.

How is Chlamydia Transmitted?

Chlamydia is easy to transmit through oral, genital, or anal sex with an infected partner. The bacteria are carried in semen and vaginal fluids. Chlamydia primarily affects the mucous membranes of the cervix in women and the urethra in men.

Chlamydia can be passed from mother to baby as baby passes through the vaginal canal.

Kissing is not a risk factor in transmitting Chlamydia, and the infection is not passed on through towels, toilet seats, bedding, or other inanimate objects.

What are the symptoms of Chlamydia?

A person can be symptom free for life, or symptoms can develop weeks, months, or years after an infection takes place.

Women may experience a frequent need to urinate, burning during urination, genital irritation, and yellowish-green vaginal discharge. In males, symptoms include a clear thin discharge from the penis, burning with urination, an itchy or irritated feeling in the urethra, and redness at the tip of the penis, with infections of the anal area,. Other symptoms may include pain, discharge, and bleeding. Chlamydia of the throat, contracted during oral sex, may produce no symptoms, or may appear as a sore throat.

What is the treatment for Chlamydia?

Once diagnosed, Chlamydia can be cured with antibiotics. In many states, a teen does not need parental consent to be tested and treated for STD.

What is Gonorrhea?

Sometimes called "clap," gonorrhea is caused by the bacterium Neisseria gonorrhea (N. gonorrhea), which produces a number of genital infections and can infect the mouth, throat, and anal area.

How is Gonorrhea Transmitted?

Gonorrhea is very easy to catch and is transmitted through sexual contact with an infected partner and thorough oral sex. The bacteria are carried in infected discharge, semen, and vaginal fluids. Gonorrhea commonly affects the mucous membranes of the urethra in males and the cervix in females. Gonorrhea can be passed from an infected woman to her infant during delivery, but it cannot be passed on inanimate objects such as toilet seats and towels.

What are the Symptoms of Gonorrhea?

A few people may experience symptoms as early as one day after infection, while some may feel nothing for several weeks. Typical symptoms of gonorrhea in a female, these include pain or burning during urination, yellow or bloody vaginal discharge, and/or spotting between menstruation and after intercourse. In males, the most common symptom is discharge from the penis and a moderate to severe burning sensation during urination. Discharge is usually yellow and heavy, although it can be clear and almost unnoticeable.

Both men and women can experience gonorrheal infection in the anal area, marked by pain, itching, discharge, and bleeding. Gonorrhea of the throat, contracted during oral sex, may produce no symptoms, or may appear as a sore throat. redness and a thick yellow discharge mark a Gonorrheal eye infection, and this is most common in newborns.

Are there complications from Gonorrhea?

Gonorrhea can also affect the abdominal area and cause pain and inflammation around the liver, a condition known as Fitz-Hugh-Curtis syndrome. Women who become infected with gonorrhea while they are pregnant run a risk of miscarriage and premature delivery. In men, complications of gonorrhea can include infection of the prostate, which causes pain between the testicles and anal area. If the epididymis becomes infected, scarring can impair a man's ability to have children and can even cause infertility.

What is the treatment for Gonorrhea?

Gonorrhea can readily be cured with antibiotics.

* Note: Be sure to take STD medication for the length of time prescribed, even if symptoms disappear,; otherwise, an STD infection can return in a more—serious form.

Gonorrhea must be reported to the Health Department. In most states to ensure that all sexual partners are contacted and receive treatment.

Syphilis?

Syphilis can mimic a variety of diseases and can affect virtually every part of the body.

How is Syphilis Treatments?

Syphilis is transmitted through sexual contact—vaginal, oral, or anal—with an infected partner. Sources of infection are syphilitic sores, rashes, and lesions, and possibly blood, semen, and vaginal—secretion bacteria. Bacteria enter an uninfected person's body by passing through mucous membranes or through tiny breaks in the skin. The microbes are easily transmitted.

Syphilis often crosses the placenta barrier and infects an unborn fetus. Almost half of untreated infected women will have a still birth (a baby dead at birth) or will deliver a baby that dies shortly after birth.

There is no evidence that syphilis is passed on toilet seats, swimming pools, hot tubs, shared clothing, or other inanimate objects.

What are the symptoms of Syphilis?

Syphilis infection is divided into early and late stages. The early stages of syphilis includes primary, secondary, and early latent periods. Primary syphilis starts at the moment of infection and lasts for several months. The first symptom is a single, painless sore termed chancre (pronounced shan-ker) The chancre is small and round with raised edges and appears between ten and ninety days (the average is three weeks). After infection, it arises at the point where the bacterium entered the body. This can be the penis or scrotum in males; the vagina in females,; or the anus, lips, or tongue in either sex.

Many people miss the initial chancre because it is painless and is often in a non visible spot. Swollen lymph nodes are found in the genital area spot. Symptoms usually disappear without treatment after a few weeks, and the infected person may never know he or she has syphilis.

Without treatment, secondary syphilis develops. During this period, bacteria enter the bloodstream and spread to other organs in the body. Persons are extremely infectious to partners at this stage and can even infect people through non sexual contact with a break in the skin. Symptoms may be similar to the flu, and can also include the following:

- : RA rash characterized by brown sores, particularly on the palms of the hands and the soles of the feet.
- : Swollen lymph nodes.
- : Sore throat.
- : Joint pain.
- : Headache and fever.
- : Hair loss.
- : Wart like lesions in the genital area.

If the disease is not treated at this point, symptoms again appear, and early latent syphilis begins. This period can last for decades and can be detected only through blood tests. During this time, however, spirochetes multiply and spread into the circulatory system, central nervous system, brain, and bones. A person is commonly not infectious during this period.

Late stage of tertiary syphilis is rarely seen in modern times for (2) two reasons. First, many people get treatment earlier in their infection. Second, 75 percent of people with long-term syphilis never show symptoms. Tertiary syphilis can damage almost any organ or system in the body. Other symptoms include mental illness (dementia), blindness, degeneration of the reflexes, vomiting, deep sores on the soles of the feet, and severe abdominal pain. Death can occur due to infection of the heart and major blood vessels.

Children who are born with syphilis (congenital syphilis) may have no symptoms, or a variety of problems that include failure to gain weight, fever, rashes, sores, bone lesions, and bone deformities. Complications such as deafness, blindness, bone pain, and deterioration of the central nervous system may appear later in life. Some typical, irreversible signs that a child has had congenital syphilis include a high forehead, no bridge to the nose (saddle nose), and peg-shaped teeth (Hutchinson's teeth).

What is the treatment for Syphilis?

Most cases of Syphilis, including congenital syphilis, can be cured with penicillin, although any damage done to body organs and system cannot be reserved. In persons who have had an infections for less than a year, a single injection is usually sufficient.

It is common for a pregnant woman to be tested for syphilis. During a routine prenatal checkup.

What is genital Herpes?

Genital herpes is caused by the herpes simplex type 2 virus (HSV-2). It is one of a family of virus that causes cold sores, chicken pox, shingles, and mononucleosis. Herpes simplex type 1 virus (HSV-1), which causes oral herpes (coreld sores), is a close relative of HSV-2. Oral herpes most commonly occurs around the face and is transmitted non sexually through kissing or on the hands of someone who touches a cold sore. HSV-1 can sometimes infect the genital area,; however, HSV-2 commonly infects the genitals, but can also infect the face, throat, and eyes as well.

The chance of catching genital herpes during a single encounter with a partner who is infectious is very high.

How is Genital herpes transmitted?

Genital herpes can easily be transmitted through unprotected vaginal or anal intercourse or through oral sex. It can also be passed without intercourse if someone simply has genital-to-genital contact with a person who is infected.

* Note=: One out of five people over the age of twelve is infected with genital herpes. Herpes migrates from the skin.

What are the symptoms of Genital Herpes?

An estimated 20% percent of people who become infected with herpes never have symptoms and never know they are infected.

If symptoms develop, these usually first arise within two to twenty days of infection. Initial symptoms may be a bump or red area, and itching, burning, or tingling of the skin. These first symptoms are termed prodrome period, and can serve as a warning to a herpes sufferer that he or she is very infectious and is going to have an outbreak. (an occurrence of blisters).

*   Note=: Herpes symptoms can occur on any area of the body supplied by an infected nerve.

The most characteristic are blisters, usually about the size of a pinhead (but can be larger), which appear alone or in clusters. These can arise on the genitals, buttocks, groin, anal area, and pubic hair region. They are often itchy, but can also be very painful. Tiny slits or painful ulcers can form when blisters burst. Blisters and sores that occur on skin surfaces usually scab over as they heal; those that occur on mucous membranes do not.

Other symptoms of herpes infection can include the following:

> Fever, nausea, chills, muscle aches, tiredness, and headaches
> Difficulty and/or pain during urination
> Swollen, painful lymph nodes in the groin
> Weakness, pain, or tenderness in the lower back, legs, groin, and buttocks
> Numbness in the genital area or lower back

Herpes symptoms normally last five or seven days, but may last as long as six weeks. They may be so slight that infected persons never realize they are having an outbreak. On the other hand, they can be very painful and traumatic, causing sufferers to miss work or school.

Many infected individuals mistake their herpes symptoms for something else. For instance, they may experience pain during urination and believe they have a bladder infection or mistake vaginal discharge for a yeast infection. They may use antibiotics or over-the-counter yeast medications and think they have successfully treated their problem because the symptoms go away. In fact, the herpes infection has just subsided for a time and has the potential to recur later.

Women tend to experience more severe symptoms than men do. Persons with weakened immune systems generally have outbreaks that are longer and more severe as well. The primary episode of herpes is usually the most severe and takes longer to heal than later outbreaks.

*   Note=: Herpes makes people more susceptible to HIV infection, and can make HIV-infected persons more infectious to their partners.

In some cases, herpes infections can become serious. The virus can inflame the lining of the spinal cord, causing viral meningitis. Symptoms include stiff neck and sensitivity to light. Oral herpes infections can cause encephalitis—(inflammation of the brain-) with headaches, fever, and seizures. Half of babies who are infected with herpes at birth die or suffer permanent neurological damage. Others can develop serious problems that affect the brain, eyes, or skin.

What triggers Herpes Out breaks?

Experts do not fully understand what causes the herpes virus to become active, but various factors seem to trigger outbreaks. These can include emotional and physical stress, fatigue, illness, certain kinds of food such as nuts or chocolate, hormonal changes related to menstruation and pregnancy, poor eating habits, trauma to the skin, or exposure to sunlight. Sometimes outbreaks occur even when sufferers do everything they can to avoid triggering the virus.

What is the treatment for Genital Herpes?

Antiviral drugs need to be started within seventy-two hours of the beginning of an outbreak to be most effective. They must be taken for ten days. If babies who are born with herpes are treated immediately after birth with acyclovir, their chances of avoiding the effects of the disease are greatly increased.

There are several steps a person can take to ensure that maximum relief is obtained from prescribed medications. They include the following:

> Keeping blisters and lesions dry, since this will speed healing
> Wearing loose clothing
> Being tested for other health problems that may be weakening the immune system

> Trying a different antiviral medication if the one being used is not providing satisfactory relief
> Making sure the dosage of medicine is correct (check with your doctor)
> Identifying triggers that may bring on an outbreak-stress, fatigue, certain foods, etc.—and avoiding them if possible.

Alternative Treatments

>Tea.

Many people have found that damp black or green tea bags, placed on herpes sores, can be smoothing. Some people believe that drinking green tea can inhibit the virus. Soaking in a warm bath in which several tea bags have been steeped can be both relaxing and pain—reducing to herpes sufferers as well.

Drying agents.

Substances such as cornstarch and rubbing alcohol that dry out the skin may promote healing of herpes lesions. Alcohol will sting when applied, however.

* Note=: Topical corticosteroid creams, commonly used to reduce itching, should never be used to treat herpes. They can make the infection worse. Ice-cold compresses or ice, wrapped in a thin towel and applied directly to the blisters or lesions, may lessen the severity of symptoms. Some people believe that ice may prevent an outbreak if it is applied during the prodromal warning period.

What is Aids?

AIDS (acquired immune deficiency syndrome) is the most complex of all STDSs. It is caused by the human immunodeficiency virus (HIV), a retrovirus that destroys the immune system—the body's natural ability to fight disease—and leaves a person open to infection and illness.

When HIV invades the body, it targets two other types of lymphocytes, the T-helper and T-suppressor cells, which regulate the immune system by controlling the strength and quality of all immune responses. HIV inserts its genetic material into the T cells, replicates inside the cells, and eventually destroys the cells as it goes on to infect others. When HIV first infects the body, a large amount of virus circulates in the system, and the number of T cells goes down.

The body's immune system is usually strong enough to suppress the virus for a time. At some point, however, the virus gains the upper hand, and a numbers of T cells start dropping significantly. It is at this point that a person's immunity becomes seriously impaired,; he is considered to have AIDS, and is at high risk of developing a variety of infections and diseases that inevitably prove fatal.

Persons who are infected with STDSs that cause sores or rashes are at greater risk for catching HIV than those who are not, since the virus passes through breaks in the skin. Women who use oral contraceptives may also be at higher risk, because changes in tissues of the cervix make cells more vulnerable to HIV infection.

How is HIV Transmitted?

HIV can be spread in three ways—sexual transmission, contact with infected blood, and transmission from mother to child.

Sexual transmission includes unprotected vaginal or anal intercourse, oral-genital sex, or other genital contact where semen or vaginal fluids are passed.

Transmission by contact with infected blood can take place in the following ways:

> Transfusions in which a person receives infected blood or blood product. Today, the risk of infection from blood is very low, since supplies are carefully screened for HIV.

> A stick with a needle that has infected blood on it. Health-care workers are at risk for infection in this manner, but their risk depends on how much virus is present on the needle and on how long ago the needle was used. A person involved in this type of incident usually has a very low risk of becoming infected with HIV.

> Contamination with infected blood on mucous membranes or through a break in the skin. Such contamination could possibly occur through acts such as "French" (open mouth) kissing, or through a sharing of razors or toothbrushes, because of the possibility of contact with blood or open sores. The risk depends on how much virus is present and the size of the break in the skin, and appears to be extremely low in most cases.

*   Note=: You cannot catch HIV by giving blood. Blood banks use a new, sterile needle for each individual donor.

Despite the widespread fears, HIV does not seem to be transmitted in the following ways:

> Sneezing, coughing, or breathing on food
> Casual contact such as hugging, shaking hands, using public toilets, touching doorknobs, sharing drinking fountains, etc.
> Contact with urine, feces, sputum, sweat, or nasal secretions (unless blood is clearly visible)
> Insect or animal bites
> Sharing work or home environments
> Donating blood

What are the symptoms of HIV and AIDS?

HIV often does not produce symptoms immediately after infection, although a newly infected person is highly contagious. If symptoms do occur, they can be mistaken for flu and can include sore throat, fatigue, fever, headache and muscle, pain, nausea and lack of appetite, swollen glands, and a rash over the entire body. Symptoms disappear after one to four weeks, and a person may not realize that he or she has been affected with HIV.

A period without symptoms follows initial HIV infection. This period may last up to ten years. Individuals are not as infectious during this time as they are in the beginning or when AIDS develops, but they should remember that they are contagious nevertheless.

When symptoms reappear—the onset of AIDS—they include fatigue, shortness of breath, general discomfort, "night sweats," persistent fever, swollen lymph nodes, diarrhea, and unexplained weight loss. Unlike earlier symptoms, these are usually severe enough so that an individual will seek treatment. The body's weakened immune system also allows a variety of mild infections such as thrush (a fungal mouth infection) and vaginal yeast infections to develop. At this stage, infected persons are very contagious due to high levels of virus in the blood.

Women with AIDS have a higher occurrence of cervical cancer than do uninfected women.

Death from AIDS is often a slow, painful, and traumatic experience both for the sufferers and for those who love and care for them.

Children who are infected with HIV generally develop AIDS much more quickly than do adults, and the progress of their disease tends to be more rapid. Many children who are born with HIV do not live more than two years. HIV infection can slow the growth of children and impair their intellectual development and coordination.

*   Note=: A person does not die of AIDS, but of complications that stem from the many opportunistic infections or cancers an AIDS patients develops.

What are Genital Warts?

Genital warts are caused by the human papillomavirus (HPV), a family of more than seventy different types of viruses that cause warts on hands, feet, and genitals.

The chances of getting HPV through a sexual encounter with an infected person are high. About two-thirds of people who have repeated sexual contact with someone infected with genital warts will become infected within three months. The more partners a person has, the greater the chances of becoming infected with HPV.

According to some experts, smoking may increase a person's risk for developing genital warts because it suppresses the immune system, allowing HPV more chance to manifest itself. In one study of almost six hundred women, smokers were five times as likely to develop visible warts than with nonsmokers.

How is HPV Transmitted?

HPV lives in the skin and is transmitted through skin-to-skin contact during vaginal, anal, or oral-genital sex. HPV is not passed through blood, semen, or other body fluids. A person can be infectious even if no symptoms are present, but the risk is probably greatest if contact is made with warts themselves. The thin mucous membranes of the vagina, vulva, penis, and scrotum are particularly prone to infection.

Babies can sometimes become infected with HPV at birth while passing through the vagina of an infected mother. There is little or no risk of catching HPV from towels or other inanimate objects.

What are the symptoms of Human Papillomavirus?

Most people who are infected with the human papillomavirus have no symptoms at all. Visible symptoms are small bumps (warts), which usually develop between thirty and ninety days after initial infection. In a few people, warts may not appear until years after the initial infection.

With genital types of HPV, warts develop on the penis and scrotum, inside the urethra, around and inside the vagina, and on the cervix of the uterus. They may appear inside and around the anus, on the lower abdomen and upper thighs, and in the groin. Occasionally, they occur in the mouth and throat, or on the lips, eyelids, and nipples. A person may never know he or she has genital warts if this condition occurs only inside the urethra or on the vagina or cervix.

Genital warts can look like regular warts. They may be flesh colored or darker, and they are usually harder than surrounding tissue. They may be flat or raised, single or multiple, large or small. They can grow and spread and assume a cauliflower-like appearance, or they may remain small and barely noticeable. They may itch, but they usually do not hurt unless they are scratched and become irritated.

Often, genital warts go away without treatment. The virus does not disappear, however. People can experience out breaks of genital warts throughout their lifetime, although the virus commonly becomes less active as time passes.

Are there Complications from HPV?

Most genital warts are harmless, but they can have dangerous consequences because they increase a person's chances of developing cancer in the genital area, particularly cancer of the penis, anus, vulva, and cervix.

*   Note=: Cervical cancer is curable 90 percent of the time if it is detected and treated in its early stages.

Genital warts not only increase the risk of cancer;, they can also cause problems during pregnancy, when they have a tendency to grow rapidly. If they enlarge, they can make urination difficult. If present on the wall of the vagina, they can cause obstruction during delivery. Infants born to infected mothers may develop warts on their larynx (voice box). This is a potentially life-threatening condition that requires frequent laser surgery to keep airways open.

What is the treatment for Genital Warts?

There is no cure for human papillomavirus.

If warts are large, irritated and bleeding, or embarrassing, they can be removed.

There are several procedures available for removal of genital warts. A doctor should be consulted to see which procedure is best, depending on the size, number, and location of the growths. Removal procedures include the following:

> Cryotherapy—freezing warts off with liquid nitrogen
> Physician-applied medications such as podophyllin and trichloroacetic acid, or prescription medications such as imiquimmod cream, applied directly to the surface of the warts.
> Electrocute (burning) or laser therapy
> Surgical removal
> Alpha interferon treatment—used when warts recur after removal by other means.

* Note: Do not attempt to remove genital warts with over-the-counter wart removal preparations. See your doctor instead.

Most people who have genital warts removed will experience recurrences.

What Is Hepatitis B?

Hepatitis B attacks the liver and can cause severe illness and even death.

Hepatitis B is one of a family of hepatitis viruses. Unlike hepatitis A, which is spread through contaminated food and water, hepatitis B is commonly passed through and exchange of infected body fluids including blood, semen, vaginal secretions, fluid from wounds, and saliva. Hepatitis C is also a blood-bornestrain that can cause severe liver damage and death, but it seems rarely to be passed through normal sexual contact.

Hepatitis B virus is a highly transmissible disease, about one hundred times more contagious than the AIDS virus. It can survive outside the body for at least seven days on a dry surface.

Those people at highest risk of catching hepatitis B are individuals who have unprotected sex with more than one partner, men who have sex with men, people who live with someone who has chronic hepatitis B, people who have jobs that involve contact with human blood, and people who travel to regions where hepatitis B is common—Southeast Asia, Africa, the Amazon Basin, the Pacific Islands, and the Middle East.

How Is Hepatitis B Transmitted?

Hepatitis B is commonly passed from person to person through unprotected sexual contact including vaginal, anal, and oral sex. Many people catch Hepatitis B while sharing drug paraphernalia with infected friends. Mothers can pass the virus to their unborn children during pregnancy and delivery.

Other possible means of transmission include the following:

> Sharing toothbrushes, nail clippers, or razors with an infected person (because of the risk of contact with blood or body fluids).

> Getting tattooed, having acupuncture treatment, or getting one's body pierced with unsterile equipment.
> Receiving contaminated blood through a transfusion. (The risk of this is rare today because blood supplies have been routinely screened since 1975.)
> Any other activity where there can be a transfer of infected body fluids through the skin, such as with a human bite.
> Kissing or having regular household contact with an infected person.

What Are The Symptoms of Hepatitis B?

People infected with hepatitis B may have no symptoms, although they will still be infectious.

For those who do show symptoms, these generally appear between one and four months after infection and can be mistaken for the flu. Symptoms then progress and can include the following:

> Achy joints
> Extreme tiredness and loss of appetite
> Mild Fever
> Abdominal pain
> Diarrhea and light-colored bowel movements
> Nausea and vomiting
> Jaundice (yellowing of the skin and the whites of the eyes)
> Dark urine

One-third of people who are chronically infected go on to develop chronic active hepatitis, which can lead to serious damage of the liver (cirrhosis), liver cancer, and death.

*   Note=: Every week, hundreds of teenagers are infected with hepatitis B.

What Is the Treatment for Hepatitis B?

There is no cure for hepatitis B, but in most cases, the infection goes away on its own. During the period when symptoms are present, doctors usually prescribe bed rest and plenty of fluids. Hospitalization is not necessary unless a person has other medical problems or is extremely ill.

A Vaccine for Hepatitis B

Hepatitis B may be incurable, but it is also totally preventable. A safe and effective vaccine—three shots over the course of six months—became available in 1982 m, eliminating the risk of infection for those who are immunized (take the vaccine).

The CDC recommends that all babies be vaccinated against hepatitis B at birth. Others who should be vaccinated include the following:

> Teens who have not been vaccinated, particularly teens who are sexually active or who practice tattooing or body piercing.
> Teens whose parents come from Southeast Asia, Africa, the Amazon Basin, the Pacific Islands, and the Middle East.
> People who use drugs
> People whose jobs expose them to human blood
> People who are partners of or live with someone with hepatitis B

Sites

STDs: What You Don't Know Can Hurt You, Copyright 2002 by Diane Yancey

Note* The book by Diane Yancey was copywritten in 2002. Some Vaccines and cures may have changed. For further information on these particular diseases, search the internet for disease addresses.

Acknowledgements

Special thanks to the people that have supported me and been there throughout this long haul.

My mother and father: McKinnley Jefferson and Annie Scott Jefferson

Grandmother: May she rest in peace Rosa Cole

Sons: Kedric, Andrew, and Waymond

Caesar's Palace co-workers

Lucky Club co-workers and customers

Xlibris Book Company

Finance: Maurice Carroll, for giving me the motivation to expand and move forward

Other finances: Pamela Jordan

My editor: Carol Zimmerman with The von Raesfeld Agency

Extra mile friends: Dock Hines, Kimberly Bratton, Delfia Bonita, and Shirley Peters

New book Production: Influent Solutions

Special thanks to my husband JD Nolen

CPSIA information can be obtained at www.ICGtesting.com
Printed in the USA
LVOW080353170613

338850LV00001B/138/P